Totally Bound Publishing books by January Bain

Brass Ring Sorority
Winning Casey
Chasing Lacey
Romancing Rebecca

TETRAD Group
Racing Peril
Racing the Tide
Racing the Whirlwind

Manitoba Tea & Tarot Mysteries
Magic, Mayhem & Murder
Movies, Moonlight & Magic
Moonshine, Magic & Murder

Sin City Wolf
Howl
Hunt
Honor
Hellfire

Collections
A Little Bit Cupid: Lovestruck

Sin City Wolf

HELLFIRE

JANUARY BAIN

Hellfire
ISBN # 978-1-80250-501-6
©Copyright January Bain 2022
Cover Art by Claire Siemaszkiewicz ©Copyright November 2022
Interior text design by Claire Siemaszkiewicz
Totally Bound Publishing

HELLFIRE

Dedication

Thank you, dear reader, for choosing my story in this busy world. I appreciate it more than you can know.

A special thanks to my esteemed publishers, Claire and Rebecca, for their awesome support and standing behind this series that I am so excited to share with all of you.

To Rebecca, my brilliant editor — as always, bless you for making my stories shine.

Many thanks to all the staff and writers at Totally Bound Publishing.

To my very own White Knight, Don. How can a simple thank-you ever be enough? It's an honor to be with you. All my love, always.

Chapter One

Amara

I ripped off my headphones and threw them down beside my computer. The terrible words from the medical thesis that I had just started to edit for a grad student made me want to run screaming into the streets.

Calm down. Breathe.

The name of the disease that had taken my mother too early mocked me. I too carried the RPS25 gene, the hallmark of ALS—amyotrophic lateral sclerosis, or Lou Gehrig's disease, and I didn't need reminding of the inevitable while I worked, though I did require the steady money from the various departments at the university that sent an ongoing stream of journal articles, papers and dissertations my way.

I had acquired the contacts during my time working in the administration department and I was grateful for them, needing to be self-employed at home to help my mom during those final months.

Crap. This moment had to happen sooner or later. I lived with the lurking symptoms every day of my uncharmed life. I thought I'd be better prepared for the inevitable. Apparently not.

"And I need a break from this," I said, jumping up from my office chair.

"*I love you, Amara!*" My parrot Rainbow began to prance back and forth on his perch, his dance moves timed in perfect sync with his words. *Talented guy.*

His colorful plumage of a deep blue head, orange-yellow chest and green cape, a hallmark of the little Lorikeet, gave my sweet baby a surreal appearance against the dying of the sunlight behind him.

Of course, I'd taught him to say, *I love you, Amara* since in my lonely existence, exacerbated by the COVID-19 pandemic raging outside, I probably would never hear the words said by an actual human being. For me, this was as good as it got. But at least the restrictions had been easing of late, meaning I could join my fellow humans once more if enticed.

My cell phone rang and I checked the number. Aw, Shay, the best person in the world to take a person's mind off their troubles...mostly because she had so much stuff going on in her own insanely busy life.

"Hey, girlfriend, what say we get all gussied up and hit the town running? I got the entire weekend free to be me! My sister's arrived this time as locally advertised. She's promising to look after Dad until the sun rises over Vegas Monday morning."

I hesitated, though I longed for some forget-the-crappy-world time. How did a person who just turned twenty-five in August manage to find her way to such a boring existence? If it wasn't for Rainbow, I'd go mad locked in my small apartment with just my computer for company.

That, and the endless line of work that needed editing with the ever-diminishing hope I might actually get to write my own stories one day. A minor in literature looked to go to waste at this juncture. "I don't know... I got this thesis due next week. I promised the guy and I can't afford a penalty for being late."

"You always finish on time, Amara. One night off isn't going to hurt. Please, I need this like the earth needs the rain, like the sun needs the stars, like the — "

"Okay, if you lay off the literary devices, I'll bite. Where do you want to meet?" I handfed Rainbow pieces of cut-up apple while we talked, enjoying the bright alertness of his rich blue-and-red-rimmed eyes. We shared the same eye color, though mine were not normally red-tinged, unless I'd indulged in too many apple martinis.

"I've been dying to try out the Glitter Palace casino. I'm hearing their karaoke bar is insane. And free drinks for the ladies," Shay said, her voice lilting with her trademark enthusiasm. "Of course, I can't guarantee I'll be acting like a lady after a few drinks, if you get my drift."

I got her drift. Shay might not be going home alone like yours truly after a plethora of Singapore Slings, her drink of choice. "If you promise me I just get to listen and not sing."

"No! Just one duet, *please*!" You can't deny your best friend one measly song. Please, please with candy cane elves sprinkled on top."

I laughed. Shay knew how to work me — hand-feed me a new image to fire my imagination. *Candy cane elves indeed. Last time it was miniature chocolate marshmallow bears.* "Fine. But only one. Now I gotta go if I'm going to have time for a shower and a bit of primping."

"Sure. Meet me at the entrance at nine. I'll be the one grinning ear-to-ear and doing a highland fling with an entire weekend off."

"That would be fun to see." I imagined my tall, thin friend high-stepping over crossed swords, her curly fair hair, the polar opposite of my extra-long ebony-blue locks, flying in the wind.

"And wear something red and showstopping."

"Maybe, if I can be bothered to shave my legs. Later."

I hit End on my iPhone and turned to Rainbow. "Can you do a night alone or should I call a babysitter?"

"Yes, *I love you, Amara!*"

"Your wish is my command. How about we see if Jeannie from upstairs is available on short notice?"

I glanced back at my computer and sighed. I loved novels that feature supernatural creatures that didn't exist...my decadent escape from my boring existence. I'd pay that debt forward one day, if I could find the time—writing a slew of genre romances featuring über-bad boys tamed by the heroines.

"Too bad vampires aren't a real thing. Not having to worry about getting sick would be sweet. Can you say fangbanger, Rainbow?"

"*Can you say fangbanger, Rainbow?*"

His words lifted my spirits. "Guess you can, sweetie." Maybe I should be more careful of what I said around my exuberant tweetie friend. Saying the wrong thing at the wrong time might end up biting me in the ass. Well, not like anyone ever visited me other than takeout service. I had them on speed dial. *And the local liquor store.*

"Time to call Jeannie." I scrolled down to her cell number and clicked on it.

"Hmm, no answer." Now what? I hated to leave Rainbow alone, thought in reality it was a common practice and it would only be for a few hours. Maybe I should cancel? But Shay seldom got a night off from looking after her dad. She deserved one. I couldn't let her down after getting her hopes up. She wasn't the type to head out on her own, no matter the brave front she always plastered on.

"How about I leave some music on? Do you want light jazz, showtunes, Christmas songs or classic rock?"

"*Christmas, Christmas, Christmas.*" Rainbow bopped up and down, seed flying everywhere. That was one thing about birds—they were messy little creatures. *Endearing, but messy.*

"Perfect. We have exactly the same taste, kiddo." I was a big fan of Christmas movies all year long. I quickly turned my iPod on and found the perfect albums, setting them to play in a loop. *Okay, time to get a move on.*

I ended up taking the time to shave my legs, wash and condition my hair and put on makeup. Drying my long hair, I debated on curling it or not, deciding in the end smooth and sleek was easier, before pulling the red number Shay had requested from my closet. Did I dare? It was over-the-top for me. Cut low and short, riding my thighs.

If not now, when. I'm only going to be young once, right?

"Okay." I approached the cage, my wrap and purse in hand, ready to head for the elevator that would take me downstairs. I'd already called for an Uber to the casino. "You be a good boy and I'll give you some peaches tomorrow."

"*Peaches now. Peaches now.*"

"No way, bud, I don't want my dress covered in fruit. Not a good look."

Rainbow was a notoriously messy eater, spilling and spitting food all over the place. But then what did I have to do other than look after him? *A good friend is hard to find.* And what was the other part? *Oh yes, a hard friend is good to find too.* I sighed again. I couldn't remember the last time I got laid.

In the lobby, I enjoyed the moment of looking good when Gary, our doorman, gave a low whistle. Everyone liked the guy. He always had a kind word to say and was full of cheer.

"Special night, Amara?" he asked, coming out from behind his desk.

"Meeting a friend at the casino."

"You be careful. Full moon's rising. Means trouble's on the way."

I shivered. It wasn't like our amiable doorman to be so maudlin. "You okay, Gary?" I glanced at him. His round face with the enviable dimples looked a bit paler than usual.

"Yeah. Not sure why I said that. Must be that song I was listening to earlier. I forget what it's called." He scratched the back of his neck. "You have a good time tonight, you hear. You meeting up with Shay, by any chance?"

"Good guess. Oh, there's my Uber now."

Gary opened the door for me, adding a small bow. "Say hello to Shay for me."

"Will do." I hurried toward the compact car, praying I wouldn't twist an ankle in my unaccustomed high heels. But sometimes a gal has to look good and flats don't do my petite frame much justice.

"Where to?" the driver asked, twisting around in his seat to give me a look.

"Glitter Palace, please."

It was a short ride and I was soon standing on the street, waiting for my best friend to put in an appearance. Shay was notorious for running late. But I totally understood. Her dad always managed to need one last thing from her, even if her sister was there to help. I glanced around. Other people were meeting up and joining with friends before heading in. It warmed my heart. Social isolation sucked even worse than being height-challenged.

I pulled a mask from my purse in preparation for going inside. I was about to slip it on when a man sidled up, his eyes glittering strangely in the light from the marquee. His glance locked with mine with the kind of supreme overconfidence I could only dream of. But something about him sent my hackles into overdrive. Every instinct said he was the kind of creature I would move heaven and earth to stay right the hell away from. A whiff of something ancient and rotten confirmed it as he passed by.

My heart slamming, I worked to ignore the off-putting effect he had on me, but I took it seriously. *Always pay attention to your gut instinct. It can save your life.* Gary's warning in the lobby came back to me in that instant. I busied myself with putting on my mask, not wanting to give the stranger any encouragement. *Go away.*

He leaned his head toward me just as he passed by, whispering in my ear. "I'll be keeping an eye out for you, inside, sweetheart. You're just my type."

I reacted like he'd spilled fire down my dress. "Get lost. You're definitely not *my* type." I held the ground, staring him down. He seemed confused by my reaction. Good. I hated being singled out by a man I instinctively didn't trust. *Women. We get to choose who we go with. It's not up to the male of the species.*

My missile worked. The guy walked off, not bothering to respond.

I took a few deep breaths to calm myself, feeling satisfied I had handled myself well.

"Hey, Amara, you're looking good, girl!" Shay said with a beaming smile as she came striding up.

"So are you," I complimented her right back. And she did look great, her curls a cascade of loveliness down her back, her midnight-blue lace dress a marvel of creation the way it hugged every curve.

"Sorry I'm late. Dad wasn't too happy tonight with me leaving." She pulled a mask out of her purse and put it on.

"No worries."

We took our time going inside, trying to catch up before we hit the casino. But we never would. That was the best part of being with Shay. Our depth of understanding of each other meant there was never an end to the conversation.

We found a choice table in the karaoke room, ordered our drinks from the friendly waitress then sat back to check out the scene. Singing was one of the few pleasures we both shared. Shay was much better than I was, but I could harmonize and keep us from looking too shabby.

"You guys here for the karaoke?" the waitress asked in a cheery tone as she placed our drinks in front of us.

"Yup. What's the money tonight?"

"A thousand dollars for first place."

"Wow, what's the occasion?" I asked. That was a lot of money for singing a song, if a person wasn't a professional. Of course, that meant the competition would be stiff tonight. We'd never win. But the entertainment value just went through the roof.

"Semi-finals and the owners wanting to get more people in here, you know, since COVID reared its ugly head."

"Yeah, I hear you."

"You don't have to wear the mask when you sing, if you have proof of vaccination on you?"

I nodded and pulled out my phone. "Here you go."

Shay did likewise and we were all set.

An icicle of dread silvered down my spine. There was that creepy guy from outside again, staring at me from an alcove nearby. The look in his eyes made me pause. It was so ancient and cruel. If I didn't know vampires weren't real, I would think this guy could be one.

I had instantly disliked him outside and the feeling was growing stronger by the second. *Stay the fuck away from me.*

I shot the idea as best I could across the room at him, narrowing my eyes with dislike. He raised his drink at me as if offering a toast. Or asking if I wanted a drink? I shook my head—a firm no—and turned away. The sense of dread that seeing him again had brought on annoyed me. I worked to keep all my focus on my friend. I was safe here, right, surrounded by a growing crowd of people?

Full moon be damned. I wasn't letting that asshole ruin my evening. An image seared my brain at that second. One of hellfire, of pain and ruin beyond belief. Then it was gone, leaving a trail of discomfort in its wake.

What the hell is up with the universe tonight?

Chapter Two

Dante

I focused my attention on the small eyepiece of the electron microscope, carefully separating the precious strands of cellular material obtained from hydra rich with the FoxO gene. Studying DNA, the source code for the most complex machine in the known universe — werewolves — was my passion. I had also single-handedly classified the entire Lycan sequencing catalog for the benefit of the species.

But I was most excited in locating the rare find I was studying at the moment, belonging to the phylum Cnidaria and the class Hydrozoa, a predatory species rich in regenerative ability. That information alone was worth more than its weight in gold and essential to my quest of extending mortality for my pack. If anyone on the planet could make this impossible dream happen, it was me with my ability to single-mindedly pursue a worthwhile goal. Of course, it would take a lot of time and effort, but didn't anything that was worthwhile?

Why should the *inmortui* species of vampires be the only ones to live past a human lifetime? And all this talk of Forever Mates and trying to find them again each lifetime — wouldn't it be far better to avoid all that and know having an extended life would allow for more scientific discoveries or other more useful endeavors than believing in having one mate that would complete us?

The door to the lab suddenly opened, making the single strand of DNA almost slip from my grasp.

"I hate to interrupt, but it's time for you to leave, Dr. Luceres. You told me to inform you when was time?" Lenore Adams, my personal assistant, said, her tone respectful but certain of her intel.

Of all times to be called away, just when I was on the verge of an important discovery. The event I had to attend was just once a year, but how quickly a year went by. I nodded at her but continued working, damned if I would stop before I saw the work completed.

I finished the essential sequencing, then whirled around in the wheeled rolling chair to observe Lenore standing and waiting with my black satchel in one hand and a slim leather folder with the itinerary in the other. She looked good, professional and yet approachable. Lenore was always well groomed, her blonde hair tidy in an upswept hairdo and her clothes clean and pressed.

We'd hooked up a few times in the past year, discreetly of course, mostly offering that essential outlet of full moon diversions from time to time. Neither of us wanted any kind of commitment, a fact that suited. Well, a werewolf had to do what a werewolf had to do on occasion, just not be a slave to it.

"Thank you for taking care of it, Lenore."

She smiled. "No worries. So, are you going to have any free time during this trip?"

Her question took me by surprise. The last thing I wanted was to bring home a female that might be misconstrued by my family. They were always hinting I needed to date more, find my Forever Mate. Right, like such a thing could exist. I'd once made the calculations of the possibility of it being a real event.

Assuming the werewolf soul mate lived at the same time as him, and they made contact, the chances were too dismal to envision. About 500,000 to 1 for supes. But better odds than humans with their far larger populations. That number would be 500,000,000 to 1 *and* that was only in one lifetime out of 10,000!

"I recall you mentioning that you were planning a weekend getaway with your sister? Have your plans changed?" I asked.

She shrugged. "Not really, but I could easily skip on Anna as she didn't sound too enthused, having recently met a new guy that she thinks is *the one*." She rolled her eyes at the very idea. We were both in agreement that statistically finding the one was a needle in the haystack. An urban legend. "But it gives her an excuse to stay home with him."

"Please, don't cancel on my account." I grimaced, expressing my displeasure at having to travel this weekend. "Bad enough I have to attend. You'd have a lot more fun with your sister, trust me. My family can be a bit overwhelming."

I got to my feet, effectively ending the conversation. Never before had my assistant suggested going *anywhere* with me, and especially nowhere near my family. She came from a different pack in the Vegas area, the House of Anche, while my home was with the most successful pack of all time, the House of Luceres.

Fortunately, she wasn't from our rival group, House of Ribelle, or I would not have hired her. I didn't need or want the complication of taking her along to the annual meeting. It sent the wrong message. I was sworn to a life of near monkhood, in my dedication to science, and it suited me just fine.

I shrugged off my lab coat and pulled on my bomber-style leather jacket with the built-in armor plates and picked up the motorcycle helmet. One sweet indulgence. Riding the wind. I knew it was statistically a bad idea. But I'd been hooked on riding Harleys since the age of sixteen, and Uncle Cesare had gifted me one over my parents' objections.

The open road was the one place I could let my mind roam free. And it paid off tenfold. How many incredibly astute ideas for following threads in the lab had happened while riding a bad boy? Even my most recent research on extending the lifetime of shifters had come about during the long ride to the Grand Canyon. I sifted, I sorted and my very capable mind pulled together diverse ideas that paid off.

I glanced at Lenore. She was biting her lower lip, like she wanted to say something else. *Please don't ruin what we have.* The reality of which was zero relationship except for business or isolated pleasures. If she was thinking differently, then even those would drop off to absolute zero. Nowhere did my life plan include a wife and children. Never going to happen. I knew my preferred limits. Not like stardust was ever going to dance in my eyes. Who needed happy? *I'm a science guy to the core.* No emotion was the way to go.

"Well, if you change your mind, give me a call. I might need the diversion." She spoke in a chipper tone, like she had it figured.

Good. Nipping problems in the bud was my preferred plan of action.

She held out my luggage and I retrieved the black leather satchel from her outstretched hands. I was packing essentials only in the Harley's saddlebags. "Thanks, see you Monday."

She gave me a look like she was expecting something else. *What?*

"Don't be surprised if we run into each other in Vegas. Anna was making noises of hitting the town. Just to give you a heads-up. I know you dislike surprises."

More than you know. "No need in this case. The Luceres meetings are always private, by invitation only. I'd say the chances of us running into each other are statistically close to nil."

She opened the door for me, and I strode through it. *Note to self — hire a new assistant after giving Lenore a raise and a promotion to head office. And next time, make sure they're male.*

I felt Lenore's eyes drilling into my back as I made my escape, descending in the elevator to the sub-basement parking level. I entered the private space blasted from rock under the large stone mansion in the Hollywood Hills that housed the private lab I'd built up from scratch.

It was pretty much earthquake and tornado-proof, an essential in LA, and obscenely expensive, but what was money for if not to grease palms and acquire all the trappings in aid of worthwhile pursuits? Hell, I could spend a lifetime and be incapable of using up even a very small percentage of the acquired wealth of my disgustingly rich family.

Inside the large garage my Electra Glide sat shining in all its perfection. The next three-and-a-half hours were going to be a rare pleasure, driving this black beauty to Vegas. It might even make up for leaving my work behind in the lab.

Stowing my bags on the motorcycle, I fired the engine to life, its power vibrating at full throttle between my thighs. I expertly directed the Harley out of the garage and down the steep hill to the canyon floor, careful to watch for traffic when I hit the main intersection that would lead me toward San Bernardino then into the Mojave Desert before striking Las Vegas around midnight. *Perfect.*

Just outside of Barstow, I directed the motorcycle onto the short side trip that led to the weathered parking lot that was home to my favorite stop between LA and Vegas, the Hot House. The weathered two-story building, pushed down and bleached pale from the desert heat, was frequented only by werewolves and never advertised its existence to the outside world, making it the perfect place to catch up on any intel essential to creatures choosing to live below the human radar.

I'd been out of the loop for months. *Too long.* Conversation, a burger platter and a cold beer sounded about right, even though I had the money to afford dancing girls hand-serving me the prohibitively expensive Almas caviar—the most expensive food on the planet at thirty-five thousand dollars a kilogram— for breakfast, lunch and dinner. Hell, sprinkle pure gold dust as decoration and still it wouldn't make a dent in finances.

Kicking downward with a booted foot, I activated the stand that held my bike upright, then disembarked, unstrapping my helmet and laying it over the handlebars. The tarmac was mostly deserted, with just one other bike and a couple of half-ton trucks in view, which was unusual. A breeze was freshening in the west, bringing a hint of needed rainfall. Dried-out tumbleweeds littered the ground, some pushed up against the adobe and wooden clapboard structure that reminded me of the building in the old Tarantino movie *From Dusk till Dawn*. Appropriate, too, except this place catered to werewolves, not vampires.

Vampires. Eternal enemies. Worse than lions and hyenas. They were gruesome creatures, according to most of my kind, living on the blood of humans, even after all the centuries of existence. What they needed was to put more stock in creating better substitutes to meet their nutritional needs. Invest in better scientific discoveries, set up labs and get to work on the matter like my family was doing, supporting my efforts to create, but no, they were all show and flash. *Pathetic really.*

I sluiced water from a bottle onto my face, letting the wind dry my skin, refreshing after the ride. Striding up to the door, I opened it and ducked my head down. A low doorframe had been installed, shorter than most for a reason. If a customer couldn't remember to watch out for it, then they were too drunk to drive. Glancing around, I noted the place was nearly deserted, which suited me just fine. It was the bartender I wanted to speak with anyway.

Julio Anche had been serving drinks at the Hot House for over a decade. More importantly, he was a wolf who kept his finger on the pulse of the community and yet kept all other cards close to his perennial black vest, black jeans and razor-sharp wit.

"Hey, Dante. Long time no see," Julio called from behind the bar where he was in the process of wiping the top of the already immaculate mahogany surface with a shine rag. "They finally parole you for good behavior?" He smirked, his blue eyes filled with a teasing glint.

"Just heading home for the yearly proof-of-life check." Referencing the demand of people who won't pay a kidnapper without the standard verification method, I found a bar stool with my name on it and sat down.

"You look good. Riding the hog today?"

"Is there a better way to journey? At least it helps with having to leave unfinished work behind." I dug into the bowl of salty nuts that Julio had laid out for me, fresh from the tin. I appreciated the gesture, not being a big fan of others digging into the same food.

"How's that going? Last I heard you were single-handedly sequencing the genome for Lycans?" Julio had moved on to polishing glasses and setting them up behind the bar.

"Finished. Been busy studying a species of hydra that has some interesting aspects this past week." I took a long pull on the frosty beer mug that Julio had also set down for me without prompting.

"Usual?" Julio asked with a rise of his dark eyebrows.

Tan from the summer sun and his love of wind surfing, the bartender exuded health and vitality, a pack member of the House of Anche who had escaped the family fold same as me a decade ago.

Setting up in LA, finding the perfect spot for the lab, had given me the space I required from daily pack dynamics to be my own man. It had been hard won, but I'd succeeded and vowed never to go back. Sure,

23

sometimes I missed the camaraderie of the fellowship of the casinos in Vegas, but it was the cost I was prepared to pay.

My time was better spent protecting my pack the best way I could — research and development in the medical field that few had paid any attention to for decades past. Staying in Vegas would have meant more social interactions, taking time away from the important work. Werewolves took their amazing constitutions for granted, never thinking that maybe it needed to be protected more. *Assisted.*

"Yeah." I waited while my old friend sent in the order, then watched him draw a beer for himself. Julio joined me, sitting down on a stool.

"Bad juju in the world tonight, bro."

I arched my eyebrow at the unexpected subject. I had no belief in such things. What couldn't be scientifically proven did not exist.

"How so?" I asked, curious what had made my normally sound-minded friend suggest such a thing. Was Julio having me on?

"You forget there's a total lunar eclipse tonight against a full moon? Everything celestial lining up — and not in a good way? Scheduled for a couple of hours from now. Midnight. It portends disturbances, problems making good decisions, havoc to all the creatures, or at least according to my current girlfriend, Nour." Julio shrugged, though his expression remained dead serious. "Maybe you should consider staying over until morning? Lots of rooms available upstairs. Great to have you. We can get drunk together and shoot the breeze."

I ignored the odd experience of a cold draft trailing its icy fingers down my spine. Someone must have turned up the AC. "Wish I could. But I got a meeting in the morning I can't miss and I don't enjoy traveling with a hangover—even on the bike."

"Suit yourself. But those bloody vamps are notorious for running amok during an eclipse. Keep your head up since you're traveling alone. I've even heard rumors that Akar I from the Old Kingdom's back in Vegas, and who know what he's after this time? Or who."

I gave a snort. "I've figured out a way to maximize werewolf endurance and strength with the use of stem cells. Better healing too. Just looking to patent it. They'd better be on the lookout for *me* since I've been testing it on myself for the past month. I can bench press double my usual—never tire out either."

"Sign me up for any clinical trials, please. My girlfriend's a wildcat in bed. The other night she nearly shredded my back. Not that I'm complaining—she leaves me more than satisfied. Just wish she was a bit more balanced in her thinking. I should have known better. Romanian pack members can be a tad dramatic. All that Dracula nonsense and feeling like they don't get their due. Life's not boring, I can tell you that."

A memory suddenly shot to the surface. "As it happens, I do remember an old case study from a Romanian university about a sub-species of the undead that was found to be unduly affected by an eclipse." I shook my head. "It wasn't taken seriously in the scientific community, but it was an interesting read." I was about to add something about being sympathetic to his circumstances, but the sudden ding of a bell announced the food was ready.

Julio stepped away to retrieve the overloaded plates, then set the platters of food down on the bar between us, steam still wafting off the crispy golden hot fries. When the fragrance hit my olfactory nerves, my stomach immediately clenched in anticipation. I dug into the first burger with gusto.

"Amazing. I don't know how your cook gets them so perfect each time I come here. I wish my chef back in LA did as well. He feels the simple American burger is beneath his notice, always concocting something that doesn't even end up looking like food. He's very fond of cold food as it gives him more time to be artistic. I'd fire him, but he's got a family so I feel obligated to keep him on." I shrugged.

"You always did have a habit of picking up strays. So, you only stop here for Bob's *amazing* burgers?" Julio's dark eyes glinted with merriment.

"It's a draw, no denying that. I'm surprised customers aren't lined up ten deep in the parking lot. What gives with the quiet day?"

"Told you. Bad juju." Julio wiped his mouth with a napkin, punctuating his remarks with a grimace. "It will pick up later, trust me, after the eclipse passes." Julio looked up as the sounds of a door banging drew his rapt attention. "Oh shit, there she is now. Nour," he stage-whispered out of the side of his mouth. "Loaded for bear. Should have worn a cup today. I knew it, what with the damn eclipse and full moon."

"What? She also part vampire or something?" I teased, riding the moment and dishing back some of the doom and gloom of earlier. In this world, away from my normally staid existence, I'd forgotten how dynamic interactions between the sexes could become. A quick thought of my assistance's unusual vibe today was set aside, Lenore was as level-headed as they come. I must have mistaken the cues.

"Don't even suggest it! Even this far removed from my pack, I can't afford those kinds of rumors. I'd have something lopped off or worse for breaking the most forbidden rule of all—no consorting with vampires."

Nour, eyes blazing with some kind of emotional turmoil, stopped about ten feet away and struck a magnificent pose, one hand perched on a curvy hip, perfect for childbearing. Lovely amber skin, bright green eyes and full lips explained the attraction for my friend. Julio probably saw his unborn children in her eyes and didn't even know it. Wasn't the perfect hip-to-waist ratio one of the precursors to attraction? Hmm, what was the name of that book about building solid relationships that my family was always suggesting to coming-of-age pack members? *Werewolves are from Mars, Shewolves are from Venus.* Maybe now wasn't the time to mention it though.

"Nour Sehorn, I'd like you to meet my good friend, Dante Luceres. He's a prominent member of the House of Luceres, a doctor specializing in genetics," Julio said, a conciliatory tone to his usually gruff voice.

"Nice to meet you, Miss Sehorn."

Her bright gaze swung my way and I swore I felt the sting all the way down my spine. Yup, relationships are just too messy for this werewolf.

"You are a doctor of medicine?"

I nodded, keeping my expression neutral. Was this going to be seen as a good thing or a bad thing in the battle of the sexes?

"You need to fix him!" She pointed one perfectly painted red fingernail at his friend who lost his tan under the onslaught of, what did he call it again? *Right, bad juju.*

"How may I help you?" I asked, curious as to her intentions. Maybe I could pick up a few pointers on what to advise my fellow brothers-in-arms when it came to the female persuasion.

"He needs the vasectomy, the tying of the tubes, snip, snip." Nour used her hand to make the scissor symbol with two fingers. Julio blanched further while his hands instinctively cupped his balls.

Okay. *Very* bad juju, my friend. It was going to be interesting how this played out.

"I'm not that kind of doctor," I said, shaking my head and trying not to laugh out loud at Julio's predicament.

She frowned. "Call the vet then."

"Nour, what is this about? We can talk about it. Come, let me get you something to eat and drink," Julio said.

"I do know other doctors, if you need a referral?"

My words were ignored by the pair as Julio carefully took Nour's arm and helped her to find a comfortable bar stool. A whispered conversation ensued and I went back to my dinner. I needed the sustenance after a day of unintentional fasting.

I kept an eye on the pair, ready to intervene if something happened. But a pair of beaming faces turned toward me as I finished my beer. I was grateful for the dialing down of the 'bad juju', just before Julio made an announcement that surprised me to the core. "Congratulations are in order, my good friend. We're getting married!"

"Married?" Had my friend lost his damn mind? The woman had been about to have him castrated. This was the problem with emotions. They made no sense. Spock of *Star Trek* fame had it correct. *Emotions are a bloody waste of time. Where there is no emotion, there is no motive* about summed it up. I'd long ago turned off the faucet for feeling too much joy, pain or otherwise, right after my aunt had deserted her family.

A very rare occurrence in a pack, but not unheard of. Which only went to prove that if they had found their so-called Forever Mate, something had gone wrong.

"Yes." Nour beamed. "We have a little one on the way! You want to feel?"

"No thanks. But congratulations are in order. May your first child be a great blessing." I spouted the expected words and stood, throwing some bills on the table in preparation for leaving.

"What? You can't go now—we need to celebrate, bro!"

I caught the pouty look of Julio's intended from the corner of my eye and it made me even more antsy to hit the open road. "I can't. I promised my brothers that I would arrive tonight." Didn't they know their statistics? Over forty-two percent of human marriages ended in divorce for first marriages, skyrocketing for second and third, sixty and seventy-three percent respectively. Well, being shifters, the odds were more on their side. Not that it had helped my uncle and a few other couples that came to mind. And when werewolves were involved, the breakups were about the messiest on the planet.

"At least stay for a glass of champagne," Julio insisted.

"Sorry, gotta go."

Within five minutes I was outside the roadhouse, adjusting my helmet. I took a deep breath of the fragrant desert air scented by the sweet taste of freedom, climbed onto my Harley and hit the open road.

Not soon enough though. Julio had insisted on asking me to be the best man and I couldn't do anything else but agree. At least they were planning a small wedding and all I had to do was show up. Well, and arrange a bachelor party. That I would need assistance with. I sighed.

Chapter Three

Amara

Karaoke night had gotten out of hand with too many people vying for the lucrative prize. I tsked in frustration and took a big gulp of my drink to ease the tension in my neck that threatened to turn into a migraine. At least we had a table and weren't lined up out of the doorway, what with social distancing measures firmly in place, right down to the cute little feet decals on the floor and arrows pointed in the correct direction.

What I really wanted to do was to call it a night, but Shay had her eye on the cash. I knew she could use it. Her dad's medication was costly and not covered by insurance. So here I sat, waiting our turn at the mike. At least she chose a decent song, *My Heart Will Go On* by Celine Dion. The movie was featured in the *Titanic*, one of my all-time favorites.

I would certainly enjoy being out on the ocean, about now. In a good sturdy boat of course. Mr. Too-creepy-for-words was still in attendance, watching the show and sending odd looks my way. *Why do some men have so much trouble with being turned down? They take it too personally.* Not every woman was ready to swoon at the first sign of a guy's interest. Good looks were just *not* as important to a relationship as a great sense of humor and a bit of humility were.

Friends first, that was one of my mottoes. I'd never met a man yet who made me want to throw caution to the wind. *Guess I'm too strong-willed for that nonsense.*

"Okay. It's finally our turn!" Shay's voice amped up about three notches with excitement, her eyes gleaming with interest. "Let's go." She grabbed my arm and I was half pulled toward the stage. Crap, *that* guy was going to see our performance. I had been praying he'd go home, but my wish had not been granted. I'd have to brazen it out and not let my friend down. I enacted a forcefield in my mind like I had been practicing, using mind magic, pushing all thoughts away but what was happening right now within a few feet of me.

Must have worked better than I expected because something totally unexpected happened. A group of security personnel surrounded the dark man I'd found so menacing and, in a flash of movement, bore him away in tight formation. Relieved didn't half cover it. Now I could concentrate on doing my best for Shay. I was going to insist on her keeping all the prize money. She was the bigger talent anyway.

We stood side-by-side on the glittery stage, mics clenched in our hands, mine sweaty, while waiting to begin. The hardest part was those few seconds before beginning when my pulse rate always jumped around like a jackrabbit's. We shared a quick smile of support I appreciated, then the light turned green to begin the music, cuing the words to flow across the teleprompter.

We launched ourselves into the haunting song with our usual bravado, seeking to feel what the songwriter was experiencing when they wrote the poetic words. The stark reminder of loss and longing when a heart must go on without their soul mate after death always touched a deep resonance in me, bringing out part of my psyche that searched for deeper answers to life.

Shay's voice and mine blended in a way that always astounded me. We sounded like one person, albeit one very powerful person, whose voice searched to reach for more than what could be seen and quantified. But then what was the human condition but always wanting something more? Or different? Not that I believed more was in the cards for me anytime soon. COVID had pretty much lowered my chances at meeting someone to hovering around zero. Well, no point in wishing for what I couldn't have.

When the last notes of the song ended, thunderous applause broke out. I blinked, leaving the cocoon of the music behind and looked around the room. Most people were on their feet and clapping. One still figure drew my attention, because he was the only person *not* clapping or cheering. Just standing there in his black motorcycle gear and staring at me with a serious expression.

He was a tall man, well over six feet, with wide shoulders and trim waist outlined by the leather jacket and black studded chaps. His dark wavy hair swept back from a Romanesque nose except for one unruly lock that fell forward on his broad forehead. He didn't look like someone who had ever cuddled with anyone in his life.

I looked into his dark brown eyes and our glances locked. Strangely, I felt no need to break free of his gaze for a few rather intense seconds. A strange desire to touch him, to see if he were real, made my palms itch. Something inside me clenched, unfurled and clenched again. I broke eye contact with difficulty. *What the hell was that about?*

"That was great! We were awesome," Shay said as we clambered off the stage, me stumbling along beside her still recovering from the odd sensation. *A complete stranger for heaven's sake.* What was the deal with that?

"I think we stand a chance at winning," I said, relieved to be out of the spotlight while I kept my eyes constrained, looking everywhere *but* at the charismatic man who I was certain was still watching me. I must have imagined the odd sensation when our eyes locked. Maybe the guy was a fan of Celine's? We had sounded good tonight. But then he hadn't been clapping or cheering, just staring. At least his vibes were good and I didn't feel threatened in any way.

"Stand a chance? I think it's in the bag, girlfriend!"

I laughed, regaining my composure and my seat across from her. "Don't jinx it."

Other contestants were nodding and smiling at us. A few looked annoyed, like we'd stolen their precious Easter egg basket right out from under their noses. Now all we had to do was wait for the final singers before the announcement of the winner. It shouldn't be long. The contest was scheduled to end by midnight.

I finally chanced a glance over to see if the man was still there, but he was not in sight. Okay, I was a tad disappointed. The guy had been super hot, all leathered up and giving off those lovin' to ride the wind vibes. I got that. There'd been many a time I considered buying a Harley Davidson, but I just didn't have the money for such toys, not if I wanted to save up for some time off to write a novel in the future.

Another drink was set in front of me and I realized Shay had ordered it when she raised her Singapore sling for a toast. I picked up mine and we clinked glasses.

"To Celine Dion for the inspiration," she said, her eyes bright with anticipatory excitement.

"To Celine. Don't get your hopes too high, Shay. Lots of great singers out tonight. The prize money has brought on the competition."

She pushed my worry away with a dismissive wave. "I can feel it right down to my toes. Things are *happening* in the universe. Oh, that reminds me, did you know there's a lunar eclipse tonight? I hope we can get to see it."

I smiled, praying she wouldn't be disappointed if we didn't win. Shay was such a good, kind-hearted person. She deserved top prize. I loved her so much. We were more like sisters than friends.

"That lunar event might explain the energy tonight," I mused, wishing the event was over and we were both back home safe and sound in our beds. A sense of unease like a rent in the fabric of the universe made me shiver. My imagination had always been set on maximum, something that might be causing the sensation of being watched again. I pretended to yawn to hide my discomfort. "This place needs more oxygen pumped in. I'm about ready to pack it in."

Shay chewed on her bottom lip. "It's only just coming up on midnight. And see" — she pointed at the stage — "there's the host now ready to make the announcement."

A sudden impulse made me grab her hand. "No matter what happens, I'll always know you were the best singer tonight."

35

She smiled and squeezed my hand. "You're as important to this duet as me. Don't forget that. Your voice is awesome, babe. I swear you have angel blood in you."

My surprise at her lovely compliment just about stopped me from hearing the host make their spiel. I turned toward the presenter to discover she was saying our names. We'd won the grand prize. Holy shit!

A couple of stunned minutes later and photos were being taken of us as the cheque and the trophy of a miniature golden mike were handed over by the perennially smiling host.

"We can share the trophy. One month each then swap work for you?" Shay half-shouted in my ear in efforts to be heard over the din.

We struggled off the stage and began hurrying toward our table, ducking and diving around the crowd that was also looking to leave. "Sure. But I insist you keep the money for your dad. No objections allowed. I'm calling a moratorium on *any* debate, just so you know."

Shay's normally placid blue eyes turned stormy as she stopped walking and swung around to me. I just gave her *the look*. Then, worse yet, they filled with tears. "Ahh, I can't accept that. You're saving up for time off."

"Your dad's health trumps my future-maybe-when-the-universe-cooperates-date. Now, let's get out of here so that we can see that eclipse if we haven't missed it already."

We hugged, then collected our belongings and hurried toward the doors, going with the flow of people headed for the exits.

"Shoot, I need to use the restroom. Coming?" Shay said.

"Good idea." The thought of needing to pee all the way home in the taxi didn't appeal even though I was desperate to catch the last moments of the eclipse. To feel the awesome power of the earth, sun and moon as they aligned in an ancient dance. *Danse Macabre.* I shivered. Why had that depressive term come up now? Being reminded of the inevitability of an end to all life wasn't exactly my idea of a lovely way to finish such a glorious night out with my best friend. I thrust the image aside and followed Shay into the ladies', out of the stream of steady traffic.

We took turns holding the wooden and gold award while the other used the facilities. About six inches high, bright and shiny, the proof of our goddess power would be perfect over my desk on a shelf. Well, during the months I had it in my possession anyway.

Finally on the street a few minutes later, we stopped for a quick check of the sky above. Damn, too many lights in Vegas — the eclipse was impossible to observe. *Duh, should have thought of that.* Many of the event's attendees were still milling about the sidewalk, jostling for their own space and rides home. The number of bodies made me uncomfortable, but I'd soon be home.

"My Uber's here. What to catch a ride with me?" Shay asked, pointing toward a black SUV waiting at the curb.

"Mine's supposed to be here any minute. You go ahead. I'll be fine."

"If you're sure?" She thrust the trophy at me. "You keep it first."

I was about to protest, but the idea delighted me too much. "Okay." Shay already had the check safely tucked in her pocket, which made it fair enough.

We shared a smile before she hurried away, jumping in the back seat of the vehicle. I was expecting a white

Smart car and kept a look out for it as I worked to keep from being jostled by people. Minutes passed and the crowd thinned.

What was taking so long? I let out a frustrated breath, wishing I had gone with Shay's suggestion even if we didn't live close together. Maybe the guy forgot? I texted again, trying to keep the annoyance from showing in my brief message to the driver. Crap. They'd gotten a flat tire. No promise on how soon they could pick me up.

I blew out a full breath. My feet were getting tired of standing so long in high heels. Feeling a bit ridiculous, standing there with the trophy clutched to my chest, I debated going back inside.

The sidewalk was deserted now. I stood under the marquee for the Glitter Palace. A multitude of lights gleamed down and reflected off the dark pavement, creating pretty patterns that buoyed my mood. I loved little lights. I'd strung them around my apartment to create a bit of magic to my environment. Suddenly, they flickered and went out. *Odd.* I glanced around. This was the only unlit place on the Strip. What was that about?

A sense of being chilled by a blast of Arctic air made me shiver. It was a steamy hot night in Vegas and certainly not cold, just a bit spooky in the shadows. Was someone watching me again?

Get inside, right now.

The words of warning pierced my skull. I scrambled to turn around on the useless shoes. Racing for the revolving door, I banged into a body, nearly knocking me off my feet.

"Careful," a male voice, low and throaty, warned.

"Sorry, excuse me," I said, trying to get around the obstruction, clutching the trophy to my chest.

A press of something against my neck made me stumble and nearly fall. Something clattered onto the sidewalk.

"Steady," the man said, grabbing my arms and helping me to stay upright.

I blinked, my vision swimming and swirling about like it had a mind of its own, unable to see him or anything else. Colder still, I shivered violently, my teeth chattering.

"Wh…at?" I had trouble saying the word, my concentration for shit.

"Let me help you. You need to sit down."

"Yes…sit."

"You've had too much to drink," he said. His scent, a mix of chemical and sharp, washed over me pressed as I was tight against his side, offensive and off-putting.

"No," I said, struggling to get away. This couldn't be happening. Right here on the Vegas Strip. But my body wouldn't cooperate, and with little difficulty, the stranger bore me away from the front of the Glitter Palace and down an even darker alleyway.

"Where…are you taking…me?" I whispered. If I could just clear my mind, and if the damn lights would come back on, I stood a fighting chance. I did know some adequate defensive moves, thanks to classes in Krav Maga that Shay had insisted we take together.

"Somewhere private. You enrapture me, my soul reaches out for yours." Then he licked my neck, like I was a melting ice cream cone. "You are so like her, my tragic, haunted Marilyn. So beautiful and alive. I won't let you go a second time."

"That's dis…gusting," I stammered, bile rising in my stomach. *Who's Marilyn?*

"No, it is the path you've been chosen to take." His words sounded haughty, like I offended *him*, when a stranger had just licked my body.

He held me upright against the side of a building with apparent ease, his eyes glittering and intense, the only thing I could see in the darkness. So bright that I could not look away. I needed to fight, to knee him in the nuts, but my legs wouldn't work, didn't follow my commands.

When he once more licked the side of my neck, all I could do was gag before something sharp pieced the skin of my throat. A horrible slurping sound followed that made my stomach pitch. This disgusting perv must think himself a bloodthirsty vampire. Why else would he assault me? *Please, please don't let me die.* I just wanted one nice night out with a friend.

After a few minutes that lasted a lifetime, he commanded in an otherworldly tone, "Drink from me. Join us. For all eternity."

He proceeded to bite himself on the wrist and pressed it tight to my lips. When the thick hot blood touched my mouth, I struggled, but it was no use, he held my head pinioned in strong hands. The salty, metallic fluid crept down the back of my throat, bringing tears to my eyes. *What the fuck!*

Suddenly he was yanked away, his hands bruising my throat in the process. I slumped to the ground, my body succumbing to gravity.

When the lights flashed on a nanosecond later, I blinked to clear my vision, then stared in disbelief. The motorcycle guy from earlier was pelting the hell out of the sicko. Using my hands to ease myself into a sitting position against the wall, I rubbed them free of the dirt and grime on my dress, feeling like a ragdoll after its stuffing had been dumped out. I touched the side of my neck, horrified at the open puncture marks my trembling fingertips encountered.

Loud growls sent fear racing down my spine and I looked over. The two warriors slammed apart, then circled each other. Mesmerized and fearful, I watched the bad guy strike out at the hero, knocking him sideways. *No.* This was bad.

Wait! Were there claws on someone's hands? Their movements became a blur of speed, impossible to follow. Loud thuds hammered against hard flesh. Were they inflicting mortal damage? Someone's leg sliced the air, seeking to cripple their opponent. Worry for the man who had come to my rescue increased the longer the fight continued. I wanted to help, but what could I do?

Finally, the sociopath managed to untangle himself from the larger, more determined man in biker black. He raced from the alley, vowing something about not letting this go.

The man knelt down at my side, his expression tightened by concern. "You're hurt." He tore a strip of cloth from his shirt and staunched the wounds on my neck.

He looked into my eyes, his so bright blue they held me in a state of wonder. I hadn't realized how beautiful he was earlier when I was singing, but I did now and breathed in his woodsy scent that made me think of open fields and green grass on a warm summer's breeze. "Did he offer you his blood?" he asked.

"Blood?" My senses reeling, I licked my lips. His gaze followed my action, his eyes turning bluer, if that were possible.

I made myself focus. "Yes, he bit his wrist…forced me to taste it. Vile and disgusting. Thank you…for stopping him."

"I'm sorry I was too late." His eyes swam with pity.

"No, no, you rescued me." How could he think it too late? I was wounded, but I wasn't raped or worse. I would live another day. Many days, if the fates were kind.

"I can't leave you here," he said, seeming to come to a decision.

"Just get me a cab. I don't live far." My strength was already returning. But maybe I needed a tetanus shot? "On second thought, maybe I should see a doctor."

"I'm a doctor. I can tend your wounds, give you an inoculation to guard against infection and disease."

I didn't know this guy from Adam. I certainly wasn't going to just go off with him, no matter how beautiful he was. Or how good he smelled. "That's okay. Maybe call nine-one-one? An ambulance is fine." I'd figure out a way to pay for it later.

"That's not a good idea."

Oh shit. Dread crept up my spine like the cold hand of a specter. Adrenaline surged into my system. Had I just fallen from the fire into the flames? *Damn the lunar eclipse.* I was spinning from everything that had happened, sensing it might very well be the harbinger of more change, and I hate change. *Act now.*

I feigned tiredness, not far off and let 'the doctor' assist me to my feet. The effects of whatever the last psycho had injected me with had dissipated, probably along with a quart of my blood. Throwing off my shoes, I crouched into position, hands raised, in full attack mode. If I was going down, I was going down fighting.

Chapter Four

Dante

I let out a breath of frustration, taking in the crouching female. It would be laughable if not so tragic. Why was she not listening to reason? Did she not realize what had just happened here? The taking and sharing of blood by a vampire heralded a great unmitigated disaster for the victim, especially one that so closely resembled his former obsession, Marilyn Monroe.

This siren with the stunning looks of the tragic movie star and a long mane of shiny dark hair in contrast to her fair skin had captured my attention as well on first glance. She had no idea what awaited her. Akar would not give her up—this was just the first clash. What had attracted me was also no mystery—she had the right hip-to-waist ratio and did look very fertile. Plus, she had an angelic voice. Not that I was looking for company, but a male can appreciate the view.

"Stop. I'm not going to hurt you." I held up my hands in dismay. It didn't help. She launched herself at me, catching me off guard. Slamming the palm of one hand into my nose, she used the other to brace herself against my chest and spin away. "Nice move. Now *stop*, I need to tell you —"

She ignored all common sense and came back at me with a high kick to my nether region.

"What the hell!" I bent over at the waist, my package so unhappy about the situation my eyes teared in sympathy. Was I going to let this small female have the better of me? My patience at an end, when she launched herself for the third time, I grabbed her around the waist, trapping her flailing limbs within my far larger ones. Her warm flesh pressed up against my body, surprising me at how good it felt, and how lovely her scent of exotic roses bursting into full bloom was. But now she was screaming her fool head off.

"Stop it!" I commanded, pressing a cautious hand over her mouth. I needed to quiet her down. What I didn't want was any of my pack brothers finding us. They would intervene in some way that I might not approve of. None of this was her fault, though she would no longer be considered human, even this short a time after being bitten.

Her change was coming, sooner than she knew. "I am trying to help you. You've been bitten by a rabid creature and you need treatment. A world of pain is coming for you that I can assist you with. Keep you safe from further harm." Using the world 'vampire' would not aid her understanding and might further alarm her.

She stilled in my arms, giving me hope that she was able to see reason.

"Are you going to be quiet? We need to discuss this with some decorum. We don't have a lot of time here."

She nodded. I took my hand away a few inches, checking if she were indeed calmer. She didn't scream but twisted around enough in my arms to face me. Her squirming about awakened something primal I'd always kept hidden. *My wolf.* The beast arose and howled, sending his song into the night sky, wanting to spring loose and run free.

What? I gritted my teeth. That *never* happened. I forced the need to change back down with a vengeance, my flesh reeling from the assault on my senses. My wolf was someone I didn't pay attention to for long stretches of time and he normally remained silent and sleeping within, only allowed out on rare occasions. I'd always fancied myself above the fray, my scientific mind capable of overriding such constraints. This new development was unwelcome and needed to be dealt with forthwith.

"What the hell is this all about? And who the fuck are you?" she asked, jerking me away from concerns of losing control over my wolf. I'd figure that out later, find a way to ensure it *never* happened again. *Keep the pack safe* was a cardinal rule.

"I'm Dante Luceres. And you are?"

"Amara St. Clair."

"Good." It was a start at least. "If I let you go, do you promise not to run away?"

"O...kay..."

"You don't sound sincere. Give me your word. I promise, I only want to help you. Didn't I drive away the beast that accosted you?" I was enjoying her soft body entirely too much. I wanted to release her but couldn't until she understood the grave matter we'd been thrust into.

"I promise. Good enough for you?"

I loosened my hold, keeping one arm around her waist. *Such a narrow waist for a full-breasted woman.* She barely reached my shoulder, yet she had been unafraid to take me on even after witnessing the level of extreme fighting between me and Akar, trying her level best to get away. *Much to admire in that.* She had courage and beauty.

"Now, I need to get home. Could you at least give me some assistance in that regard?" she asked, straightening her clothing.

One rounded bosom had popped loose of her top after her struggles. Her budded nipple focused my eyes downward, making me incapable of answering her question. I imagined taking it between my lips and suckling, nuzzling her warm flesh. My cock stiffened with agreement, my wolf edging me on. The aroma of arousal in the air, hers and mine co-mingling into an intoxicating scent cloud of desire straight from a textbook on pheromones wasn't helping.

"Excuse me. Are you listening to me? I'm up here." She gave me a stern look while she tucked her breast away. I noted the flushed skin and the larger pupils, obvious signs of her arousal.

"Nice dress," I said, licking my lips. Then I realized what I'd done when she gave me a look through eyes that screamed *perv.* What the fuck was the matter with me? The female had just been bitten by the most loathsome of all species. I should be repelled by her, urgently needing to check the literature on the subject. Had this ever happened before? It didn't seem likely, but there had to be some kind of scientific explanation.

I needed to figure this out, ASAP. To get a grip on this insanity before it spread.

"We need to go." A heightened sense of impending danger made the hairs on the back of my neck tingle and my wolf growl. The cold one would be back, with reinforcements. This was no time to start a war. My brothers would disown me if I let that happen. *Protect the pack.* Never had those words made more sense.

"That's what I said." She gave me an exasperated look.

I took her hand and began to hurry her along the alleyway, toward the back of the casino.

"Wait! We're going the wrong way."

"My Harley's out back. Quickest way out of town."

"I'm wearing a dress. And I'd prefer an Uber or cab. No offense, but I don't know you." She jerked her arm to pull away, but I hung on.

"You're in mortal danger. I'll figure out the explanation for all this"—I gestured between us—"later when I have access to records and blood testing."

"Blood tests? What are you talking about? And why does it affect you?"

She exaggerated my hand movements demonstrating the connection between us back in my face. I did note that her hand also trembled, causing an odd emotion to come over me. She was trying to be brave, but it was costing her.

"Are you suggesting that you are not in touch with your obvious physiological responses?" Anything was possible in this alternative world she'd just had thrust on her. Perhaps she wasn't aware she had become aroused. Or refused to admit it. It didn't matter, neither of us would be acting on it in this lifetime.

"You don't understand. That beast that attacked you? He's coming back, and he won't be alone. I have to get you away right now." I added a sense of urgency to my tone in efforts to persuade her.

She did look around with a more constrained expression, as if the bogey man was going to jump her.

"Don't worry. I won't let them take you."

"Why would they take me? That makes no sense." She had the cutest way of wrinkling her nose that made it wiggle a bit.

"You look like a movie star."

"Yeah, right!" Now she gave a grimace as if I were fucking around with her.

"Yes. Marilyn Monroe. Only with dark hair. In a blonde wig, you'd be able to pass for identical twins. Your features, perfectly aligned and symmetrical, are above average in scope and dimension."

I pointed at her face, as if drawing with my fingers in the air. "The distance between your eyes is one exact eye, the length of your face equals three noses. Space from the lower eyelid to the upper eyelid is the same as space between the upper eyelid and eyebrow. Also demonstrated to perfection. And width of the face across the cheeks is equal to two lengths of the nose. Finally, eyebrows begin on the same line as the corner of the eye nearest to the nose. There you have it, a perfect oval face!" I always appreciated sharing such proof positive.

Instead of thanks for pointing out her perfection, what did I get but a rolling of her eyes before she burst into gales of laughter?

"Is that the line you try on women to get them into bed, by any chance?"

I raised my eyebrows. "No. I'm merely pointing out facts. As it happens, I've never needed to persuade a woman into sharing my bed. When the time approaches for a necessary mating—"

"*A necessary mating*?" She had begun to hiccup, her voice rising higher in pitch. "You're kidding, right. You must be the nerd of your family. How did this happen? Am I dreaming all this?"

Shock had to be setting in. Her skin appeared paler and her forehead was beading with sweat. "We need to get you out of here."

We had reached the parking lot and stood by my motorcycle.

"If you think I'm going anywhere with you on *that* thing—" She pointed with disdain at my beloved Harley.

A sudden implosion of faint sound only supernatural entities could hear told me we had tarried too long. Damn it! The cold ones were already manifesting themselves not fifty feet away. Six of them. Dark and menacing, and stalking toward us in tight fighting formation before they began to stretch out, preparing to surround us.

"Get on the bike! They're here!" I commanded. Kindergarten time was over.

She glanced over where I was looking. Without another word, she climbed on behind me. I started the motor and slammed the bike into gear, preparing to mow anyone down who stood in our way.

Chapter Five

Amara

My feet moved before my mind could form the word. *Run.* I yanked up my dress and jumped aboard. I grabbed hold of his waist and he gunned the engine. The back tire left the ground as the bike spun out. Too much gas! *Oh, my lord, we're going to spill.* Right into a pit of vipers.

Then Dante responded, shifting his weight, the tire grasped the pavement and we were flying through the fast-diminishing space between two of the menacing men in black. Would we make it? One elongated hand reached out to grab me. He missed by the smallest of margins, his cold fingernails grazing my upper thigh. The touch sent an icicle of fear stabbing through me. Worse, the piercing intensity of his red eyes that flashed as we raced by him with inches to spare would penetrate anyone's armor. Now I knew how real fear paralyzed.

We hurtled down the Strip flat out, Dante driving like a *Mad Max* character, dodging vehicles, me holding on for dear life, unable to look away. The wind tore at my hair, whipping it all about. All I could think about was how my normally humdrum life had turned on its head. But deep down, I was loving it, this adventure like no other. I was on the high seas, surrounded by possibilities and excited beyond belief.

That I was shocked to discover this about myself didn't begin to cover it. My body felt electrified, every cell supercharged. On the cusp of something I couldn't give a name to. Or explain. *Me*, the one who normally hated change, had undergone a metamorphosis in the space of an hour.

The bike slowed after a while and Dante pulled off onto a designated rest stop by the side of the interstate.

"Do you need a break?" he asked. The way he looked around constantly, keeping a continuous check on things, did not give me the confidence to linger.

"No, I'm good." Could those assholes still be following us? I didn't want to voice the thought aloud, not wanting to jinx us.

He nodded and pulled a helmet out of one of the saddlebags and slipped it on my head, fastening it under my chin. "We need to keep you safe."

"What about you?"

"I'll be fine."

"Where are we headed? I have to get home soon. I have a parrot, Rainbow. He needs a lot of attention." Not to mention my work had been left unfinished. Such mundane thoughts after our wild escape seemed weird.

"Soon as we get to my place in LA, I'll make some calls."

"Maybe we can go back now? I'm sure those men have given up. I mean, really, it's silly to think someone I don't know, even if I look like this Marilyn character, would pursue this any further."

"You have no idea what they are capable of. What *you* will be capable of soon." He shook his head. A dark shadow crossed his face, giving me pause.

Again with the cryptic talk. "What's that supposed to mean? I'm fine."

"Soon as I get you to LA, I'll explain. Can you hold on? Those men are following us, I'm certain of it."

I glanced around, more nervous now. But the rest stop was deserted, no other vehicles parked on the lot. Not even a trucker was in sight.

"This is beyond crazy. I think if we take the side roads, and slip into Vegas quietly — "

"That will never work. Akar will find you, stake out your home…wait for his chance in the dead of night."

"Wait. You *know* the man?"

"Yes. A deadly psychopath. You don't want to get mixed up with him. He'll turn you into his slave."

"You're kidding right?" Adrenaline flooded my system. The ground beneath my feet shifted, destabilized, a crack opening wide to an alternative reality.

"I wish. We need to go if you're capable of it." He gave me a searching glance, his expression grim.

"What are you checking for?" My skin began to warm under his perusal. I ran a hand through the tangles of my hair, tucking it inside my dress to stop the wind from totally trashing it.

"You look fine. Can you ride?"

What choice did I have? It was Dante or this supervillain called Akar. At least Dante was concerned about my safety, giving me the one available helmet.

I climbed back on the bike without another word spoken between us.

He did the same, gunned the motor and we were off. The minutes slipped by. Riveted to the undulating landscape of the darkened valley with only the stars to guide us, I breathed in the arid odor of the desert floor, a miasma of stirring creatures and slow-growing vegetation that held its secrets tight. There was also the invigorating scent that wafted off Dante when the breeze hit just right.

My head began to spin. His fragrance stirred my interest, sending signals to my loins. The throbbing of the powerful motor between my legs with just the delicate silk of my panties to cover myself made my need all that more intense. A chain reaction of earthquake proportions hit front and center. I admit it, I got my rocks off on that damn bike, riding behind the big man, my body pressed to his. Not once, but twice before we again hit civilization on the edge of LA.

We slowed down a bit on the canyon roads that serpentined through the hills of Hollywood. The sight of all those elaborate mansions as we climbed higher and higher into the stratosphere made my mouth water. Then a door opened up on a stone-clad castle-like structure and we were out of the dark and into a fortress. The walls had to be thick, because all traffic noise vanished as the door reseated itself.

Dante killed the motor and kicked out the stand, disembarking the bike. He held out his hand and helped me off, the touch of his warm fingers on mine a comfort after our narrow escape although nearly forgotten during the exciting ride to freedom. *Or is this freedom?* I suddenly realized I was in a confined space with a man I barely knew and tugged down my tight skirt to cover myself. Sure, he'd saved me from a situation that made no sense, but still, a woman had to protect herself.

Confused didn't begin to cover it.

"Come. You need treatment," he said, his expression concerned.

"I think it's going to be okay. It doesn't hurt or anything," I said, touching my neck. In fact, the wound seemed smaller, the pain almost gone as I probed the edges.

"It soon will," he promised.

"What do you mean?"

"Best I show you." He opened the door to the main building and ushered me inside.

"Do you have help here?" I asked as we entered an elevator.

The place was ginormous, that was apparent. But now with just the two of us in such a confined space, I could find no place to rest my eyes, Dante filling the eight-by-eight box with his huge presence. I pressed my lips together, my body far too aware of his. To keep my mind busy, I began to run my fingers through my hair to ease out the knots. I could only imagine what a sight I must be.

"I do. It takes a number of people to keep this operation running smoothly. You'd best stay away from them though for now, keep a low profile."

"Why?"

"I'll explain everything once we get you situated."

The elevator doors opened to reveal an opulent foyer. Beyond I could see a series of doors around a center courtyard that was encased in glass and filled with growing plants and trees, like a conservatory. It was amazing. Filled with not only the lush vegetation, but flitting butterflies and small birds that chirped with abandon. And what looked like a pond teemed with fish and aquatic creatures below a cascading waterfall. The heady fragrance of the jungle atmosphere refreshed, giving my senses wings.

"This is your home? You get to live here? In this sanctuary?" I turned disbelieving eyes on my host, certain I had arrived in paradise. Or Eden. The guy must be richer than I'd imagined. Not just blessed physically. Well, other than those nerd overtones that I actually thought endearing. I mean, what man knew the exact proportions of a human face? An unusual compliment, to be sure, but one that was truthful, based on science and all.

"Yes, the natural world helps with my research. Modern science is again paying more attention to what is readily available, like the best alchemists of old. I make good use of this space, both technically and spiritually." He seemed relaxed, like this was his element.

"I envy you. Living like this," I said, widening my arms to embrace the world I was viewing.

"It is good for the soul to bring nature inside. Perhaps you will want to spend time there after your recovery?"

"You keep saying that. What recovery? I'm fine."

He grimaced. "You will understand more in time. The next forty-eight hours will tell the tale."

"What? I can't stay here for two days! Rainbow needs me."

"I'll have him brought to you. He'll be here by morning along with anything else you need. In the meantime, you must rest. Come. I'll walk you to your suite."

But before he could, a young woman appeared, polished and professional at first glance in a white skirt and black pencil skirt. The only proof she'd probably just gotten out of bed was a lock of thick blonde hair that had slipped from her pulled-back hairstyle to dangle down her neck.

"I'm sorry, Dante, I didn't hear you come in. You're home a day early. Oh, you have company?" She stopped short when she caught sight of me, giving me the once over, as if checking out the competition.

So, that's the way it is. Don't worry, I'm just traveling through.

"Thanks, I've got this, Lenore. It's only just after five a.m. I didn't mean for you to be on call at this time of the morning. I thought you'd gone to Vegas to visit your sister this weekend?"

Dante looked more confused than anything by her showing up. Maybe even a touch annoyed?

The woman blushed, the expression in her doe eyes giving the game away. She adored her employer. She'd been waiting for him to come home. Dressed as fast as she could to catch him.

"Something came up and I ended up staying over last night working on some research. It's no trouble. Honestly, I can see to her." She pointed with a curt nod of her head in my direction like I was chump change.

"No. I've got this."

She hesitated, expecting to be introduced, no doubt, her mouth firmed in a straight line, then made an about-turn and vanished when none was forthcoming.

Dante took off at a brisk pace and I had to half run to keep up.

"I hope this will do?" he said, holding open a door for me.

"Oh my, it's stunning."

A high ceiling with gold leaf applied to the ornate scrolling, cozy fireplace, plush rugs, four poster bed that looked suspiciously like it had been built for the Palace of Versailles. Paintings of opulent landscapes by famous artists gave a peek into another world of endless beauty and charming visages. A history that most likely only existed in the painter's mind. *When did real life ever look so serene?*

"This is the Marie Antoinette suite. I thought you might like it. I can't really take any credit for the décor. It was here when I bought the place. I wanted a safe location in LA and this place had a lot of built-in features that saved extensive renovations. Reenforced cement concrete, metal shutters for nightfall, a safe room that can withstand high-velocity projectiles, well beyond the norm and mostly hidden under the façade. The former owner was an ex-diplomat from Russia who was paranoid and had a love of history — hence the furnishings. You should see the suite of rooms he built for his wife that mimic the Winter Palace, complete with Faberge eggs."

He seemed cheered by my reaction. He was either a man with an unlimited bank account or mortgaged to the hilt. I gave a quick prayer that I would keep my head in this situation, considering the history of the tragic French queen.

"Scientific research must pay big dividends," I said.

"Hmm, that and very old family money."

"Wait! You said earlier that you're a Luceres...you mean like the group that owns the Vegas Strip?" My eyes popped open, making the connection.

"Not all of it," he said with a smile. "But the Glitter Palace is ours and some of the other properties."

"Lucky you."

It certainly explained the humongous mansion and the expensive art work on the walls.

"Most of the time. Other times being part of such a large extended family causes difficulty. I was only in Vegas due to my presence being insisted upon on penalty of expulsion of said family." He shrugged. "I maybe exaggerating, but not by much. I've worked hard at being my own person and need to call my own shots. Though I had a good friendship with my only brother, Alejandro, growing up, it's a little less since we've both taken different paths in life."

"I always wished I had come from a larger one. Mine is miniscule, just me and Rainbow."

"You're all alone in this world?" He stilled, a frown creasing the smooth skin of his forehead. I attributed the perfect tan to LA and his love of motorcycling. He didn't appear like a man who would waste a second in a tanning booth.

"I have good friends. Shay, the woman I sang with, for one. We won the singing competition, by the way. Oh no, I just realized I lost the precious trophy tonight. And my shoes."

Then the lovely view around me disappeared and I was back being attacked outside the casino. The dark evil presence was once more slurping on my neck. I swayed back and forth, a rush of something fiery coursed through my body, making me dizzy. "I need to sit."

He was suddenly at my side, helping me to the bed and laying me back on a nest of pillows. "I told you this was coming."

A sense of outrage filled me. "What the fuck are you talking about? No more riddles. Explain now!"

He sat down beside me, the weight of his substantial body making the mattress compress under us. I focused all my attention on his face, trying to stop the sense of being on the open seas. *Vertigo sucks.*

"I'm sorry this is happening to you. It's going to be hard for you to understand this, but I will try my best." He didn't touch me, but the heat of him radiated outward, warming me. Lying down was helping — the room had stopped spinning.

"That person that accosted you, he's got a sickness that's contagious, spread through the sharing of blood."

"You called it a rabies-like virus earlier? Is that why he attacked me, because of the virus? Crap, I feel like I'm in some kind of zombie apocalypse movie."

He gave a snort. "Akar wouldn't appreciate the comparison."

"That's his name? Akar?"

"Yes, Akar. He comes from a very old dynasty of Egyptian heritage."

"Too bad about his sickness, but it doesn't excuse his actions. He should be in jail."

"No jail can contain him and his kind."

I didn't like the sound of that. "Does this mean I'm going to turn into a bloody psycho zombie like him? Can you stop it? You said you do research here. Please, is there anything you can do to stop the infection?" If it was some other part of me than my neck that had been bitten, I'd cut off the offending limb about now to avoid such a dire outcome like that brave old man in the TV show *The Walking Dead*.

"I wish. All I can do is ease your symptoms."

At least that was something, with me not being a big fan of pain. Worse yet, was I going to turn into a monster, harming those I loved? I couldn't voice the thought aloud. It made me want to puke my guts out and throw myself out of the nearest window — well, if it wasn't indestructible. As big as the place was, I felt the walls closing in.

"We can manage this condition, keep you from attacking others."

"Does the government know about this? If not, we need to warn them —"

"The infection is as old as human beings have walked this earth. No government is capable of handling this."

"Explain it to me," I insisted. "How does this virus work?"

"The spike proteins of the vampire contagion, similar to the SARS-2 virus that caused COVID-19, binds to a protein on the surface of human cells. It initiates the process that results in the virus being internalized into a cell. The virus then releases its RNA and uses our genetic machinery to reproduce itself, which releases more viruses into our bodies until it's finally too overwhelmed to fight back. Then a human becomes a vampire, having succumbed to the 'death virus'. I've found it can take hours or days, depending on the strength of the host's immune system."

"Way over my head." I stared at him in disbelief, ignoring the scientific for action. "Surely once people find out about this it can be stopped. Start a campaign on social media, raise awareness —"

"Not going to happen. It's forbidden."

His calm acceptance made me want to lash out, run screaming through the streets. "But that's crazy!" I swallowed the bile that rose in my throat, sensing an unease, a difference in my body from just a few minutes ago. I began to tremble, not sure if it was shock or the disease progressing.

"I need to get you some medicine. Will you be all right here while I retrieve it from the lab?"

I nodded, not trusting myself to speak.

He pulled a cover off the end of the bed and draped it over me, tucking it around my prone body. Then leaned down and kissed my forehead. "Rest. I'll be back shortly with what you need."

I looked into his warm brown eyes, the tenderness and pity residing there almost my undoing.

Chapter Six

Dante

I hurried to the elevator to descend to the lab, my only salvation in the catastrophic circumstances surrounding this night's tragedy. Only there could I think how to help the lovely young woman under my direct care. Amara had no idea of what awaited her. *Fuck*. Why did she have to resemble that movie star? It was the only reason Akar had bitten her, to get her to become like him and live with him all the rest of eternity.

Of course, he already had a few 'brides' as the cold ones liked to call them, the women they were attracted to, uncaring that polygamy is just as wrong for vampires as for humans, at least in my opinion.

If it ever came to it, I'd be a one-woman man. If I ever felt the need to mate one day. But my life had taken a different direction than most werewolves, the wide-open field of science that satisfied my intense need for purpose.

But to my chagrin, soon as the elevator doors opened, there was Lenore, her blonde head bent over a beaker she was withdrawing a vial of liquid from. She looked up soon as I entered, her expression serious, the last person I wanted to see at the moment. I cursed myself for not firing her when I'd had the chance the last time I'd felt uncomfortable with her over-dedication to the job and zeal for my personal life, never giving me a moment's peace.

I had to keep this whole mess quiet. She'd looked suspicious earlier when she spotted Amara. Yes, there was the stink of vampire on her, no hiding that, even though I'd hustled her away. If she guessed Amara was actually going to transition to vampire, I had no idea what she would do. Or who she might tell. Secrecy was crucial.

"I'm working on those tests you ordered the team to do. Thought I'd get an early start before the rest of the crew arrives," she said.

"You didn't need to do that. It's not in your job description. You're a personal assistant, not a lab worker." I heard the sharpness in my tone, and dialed it down. "I do appreciate your dedication, but it's unnecessary. The team can handle it. Why don't you take the day off? Go out and do something fun for a change. I won't need you this week anyway."

"I'm fine. I need to work. Who is that girl?" She glanced up from her work and gave me a quick appraisal.

"Not important." I needed to get her out of the lab. Once I started to assemble the cocktail to ease Amara's symptoms, she would suspect something if she didn't already.

I went over to her and took her by the elbow, desperate to move things along. "I insist you take the day off. You look exhausted. In fact, take the week, I'll pay you to take some vacation time. How does time in the Bahamas sound, or in Venice? You always said you wanted to have a gondola ride? Anywhere you want to go, I'll foot the bill, then you can come back all nice and refreshed—"

"No thanks." She cut me off.

I ran my hands through my hair, scraping it back from my face. I wanted a shower and had a ton of things to consider to aid Amara. Lenore needed to be gone. *Now.*

"I'm sorry, this isn't working out for me. I need my personal space." I disliked sounding brisk, even if it was the truth.

"What? Are you firing me? Is that what this is all about?" She narrowed her eyes, jumping to conclusions. "That girl. She's recently been around a vampire. And she's human. Did something happen between you? Is that why you want me gone?"

"For heaven's sake, Lenore! Nothing's going on. I shouldn't have hired you in the first place is all. This is all my fault and I apologize if you've been thinking differently than we discussed at the beginning of your employment."

I'd wanted a male assistant and should have said no right from the start, but she had such an excellent resume and had pleaded her case, saying how very interested she was in the scientific research I was known for among the shifters. And I was a sucker for anyone wanting to learn more. But I should have realized when she said we could be 'fuck buddies' once she was working for me that it might lead to complications. My own damn fault.

She trailed a red-painted finger down my chest to caress me, her voice descending to a purr. "But we have such fun together. You don't want to give that up? I know I don't."

I pulled away, floored at her behavior. Until today, I'd have said it wasn't possible, that Lenore was a sensible girl. One who knew the score.

"I'll pay you enough to set yourself up for life. A life lived in complete luxury. Anywhere you want." It was a last-ditch effort and I knew it.

"It's not about the money, honey. I want to be by your side. Meet the family. We have a good thing. Why spoil it?"

If I fired her now, I could never be sure of what she might do. Who she might go to and plead her case. All the cash in the world couldn't help this situation. I cursed myself again. I had a fragile female needing me to make her world right and I'd allowed myself to be lured into this mess with Lenore. How could I have missed the signs? But I knew how. My head always bent over an experiment, assuming others had the same dedication in mind. Until this moment, I'd have sworn she also shared my love of the scientific, that her main reason for being there was studying the process to lead to discoveries.

"You knew the score from the beginning. I don't intend to *ever* take a mate and have a family. I made that abundantly clear right from the start." She'd only been working for me for a few months. When had she changed? Or did she have this agenda right from the get-go? Is this why the family had asked me to take her in? Hoping I'd relent and accept her for my mate? My mother was always going on about grandchildren.

"Yes. But things can change. I fell in love with you, Dante. I have no control over that. Say what you will, but I think you feel it too."

I took her hand and pulled it away from my body. "I'm sorry. I don't feel that way about you. Yes, I do admire your work ethic —"

"My work ethic!" she half-screeched in my ear.

"I apologize if my words offend you. But I have urgent work to do. If you'll excuse me?"

I'd had enough. What more was there to say? I'd never tried to pretend this was anything more than it was. Yes, I wished now I'd been smarter, not accepted her terms of not wanting anything more than a jump in the hay. *Definitely learned a life lesson.* This situation could *never* be repeated. I'd keep myself free of such possibilities in the future, suppressing my own physical needs, even if I had to develop a specialized cocktail to dampen down my libido. Whatever it took.

The struggle within was obvious by the micro-expressions that passed over Lenore's face before she slammed them down into a cold stare. "I've got things to do as well," she said in a quieter tone. Relief at her words was followed by a twinge of worry that it had been too easy.

But I admired the way she sucked it up and seemed to have regained her dignity. Maybe things weren't as dire as they had first appeared? Though the fact remained that I still needed to get her out of there. No way would I ever consider having her hauled away by security, though the thought did cross my mind. This situation was all my fault and needed to be navigated carefully and properly. Lenore deserved to be treated with respect, misguided as she was.

"You know, I'm famished for one of those chocolate croissants from that bistro on Tenth and I'm certain the team would appreciate the offering. Would you want one as well?" Maybe she'd pick up on the hint? It was in her job description.

"Of course. I'll head out right now and pick up a few dozen. Be back in a jiff."

"Thank you, Lenore."

"No thanks necessary. It's my job as your personal assistant to see all your needs are met." Her tone remained neutral, which I was relieved to hear.

Then I had a moment of inspiration. The clock ticked incessantly over Amara's situation. I imagined her beautiful body wracked by pain and it was all I could do not to throw caution to the wind and escort Lenore from the lab myself. "If you're going out anyway, perhaps you could head over to Vegas and pick up a parrot?"

"Vegas?" Her eyebrows flew upward in surprise.

"Yes. Take the helicopter. Call Andrew, he can pilot it for you. You can be back in a couple of hours. I have the address on my phone. I'll text it and alert the landlord you're coming."

"No need. I can handle it. Anything else?"

"No, that's all for now. I'll text you before you land if anything else pops up. And thank you."

"It's my job. One I would like to keep by the way. Just so you know, going forward, I won't bother you with anything beyond the professional. You made it abundantly clear that is what you'd prefer." Her flat tone of voice and glittery eyes gave me pause, but I had no time to translate it.

"One more thing. I would prefer that you not mention anything about the woman you met earlier staying here. She'll soon be gone anyway."

"No problem. I am well aware of how easily you can dispose of people."

The zinger hit broadside, making me wince. My intentions were never to hurt anyone. How had I made such a mess of things? Am I the monster she accused me of being? The thought didn't sit well and gave me a moment of doubt. I'd always considered myself a compassionate shifter. One wanting to help others, and now I was being accused of being uncaring. An uneasiness sensation that settled in my gut made me want to get back to work, forget this encounter ever happened. The demands of science I understood, not the complications of females.

She finally picked up her things and vacated the lab, the dutiful employee. *Thank goodness.* I headed straight for the shelves that held the necessary supplies and began choosing the items with care. It was an ancient recipe, known by only a handful of others worldwide, and it would be mixed with the modern painkiller mix oxycodone and paracetamol, the perfect way to reduce her discomfort short-term.

Twenty minutes later, the elixir was prepared. I strode from my workspace with a few vials filled with the dark green liquid and a few sterile syringes in a small wooden box that secured the items safely, heading for the Antoinette suite.

I knocked on the door, waiting for Amara to bid me enter. But no answer. Frowning, I pounded louder. Still no reply.

"Amara, are you all right?" I spoke louder than I wanted to, worried that someone from my staff would become curious and discover my new guest. I wanted to keep the situation quiet.

Uncertainty whether to just barge in or not made me hesitate. Then a low moan that only ultrasonic hearing could catch came from inside the room. I thrust open the door, horrified to see Amara in the throes of some kind of fit, her body thrashing about on the bed, her eyes rolling back in her head.

I flew to her side, worried she was going to harm herself.

"Amara! Can you hear me?" I took her by the shoulders, trying to get her attention. But her body shook uncontrollably, her complexion pale and waxy. Looking frantically about, I searched for something soft to place between her teeth to avoid her breaking them. Nothing useful nearby. I'd have to rectify that. *Prepare better.*

Then my touch seemed to help and the tremors lessened by degree until only a stillness remained, enough that her eyes opened to stare into mine. Such beautiful eyes, like the color of periwinkle flowers. *Not very scientific,* I chastened myself. *Right, they belong to the dogbane family, scientific name Vinca minor and are native to central and southern Europe, from Portugal and France north to the Netherlands and the Baltic States, east to the Caucasus, and also southwestern Asia in Turkey. In the United States they —*

"Dante." She breathed out my name, sending tingles of pleasure through my system and nearly making me forget my intentions to never get close to another woman for as long as I lived. But she was my patient too and caring for her was more important than anything else. She was such an innocent in this situation. My heart broke for her. All alone in the world with no one to call, while I had an entire clan that would back me up in a nanosecond, with just a word.

"Be still, Amara. Your body's rejecting the venom and it's overwhelming your system. I've got something to ease this for you. But I need to inject it. Are you okay with me doing that? I need your permission."

"I trust you."

Those three words hit me hard and I had to take a deep breath to steady myself. I filled a needle with the liquid from one of the vials, then set it aside.

"I have no idea why? But you did save me in Vegas," she continued. She rubbed her forehead, her eyes glazing over. "I still can't believe what happened. It doesn't feel real."

"I understand. It's a lot to take in." I picked up the syringe again. "It would be best placed in your posterior, but if you prefer, I can use your upper arm?"

"My ass is fine." She rolled onto her side and lifted up the hem of her dress, exposing her lace panties.

"That it is," I said, surprising myself with the flirting. *Crap, Dante, the girl doesn't want her maximus glutinous admired at the moment, even if it is absolute perfection.* I could only imagine those pretty rounded globes being kneaded by my large hands as my cock—

I grunted, waking myself from the insane stupor viewing her butt had placed me in, the sweat pooling under my armpits. *Blame it on the wolf, ready to play at a second's notice.* It wasn't her fault either that my wolf was overreacting, most likely because he'd been ignored for most of his life and was now rebelling with such a thrilling enticement before him.

I tugged at the waistline of her panties and slid them down over her curvy hip enough to apply the alcohol swap to sterilize the area. With the utmost concentration, sweat dripping in my eyes, I applied the needle, careful to take the time to avoid any more pain to her.

I patted her fine ass then jerked my arm back like it had been burned. "There, all done. You should have some relief from the pain shortly." Was it my imagination, or did my voice sound gruff?

"I hope so. It feels like needles and pins are stabbing at every cell I possess." She groaned, lying back on her pillows and pulling the covers up.

That didn't help—her incredible body was a memory burned forever and a day into my retinas. "You need to rest. Are you hungry? Thirsty?" I asked.

Suddenly she began to shiver, her teeth chattering. "I'm so cold. Please, hold me," she begged.

I didn't need to be asked twice. Throwing off my shoes, I climbed in beside her, pulling her tight against my warmth. My arms felt so right around her—she was the perfect size for me. Breathing in her unique scent, my body tingled all over as every nerve ending I possessed came alive. Snuggled down with Amara, I couldn't imagine a better place to be. Well, except between her thighs. *Crap. Stop thinking about sex. The girl is in pain.*

Her body quit the reaction, and she settled in close to me as we spooned on the giant antique bed fit for a king and queen.

"This is nice," she said before promptly falling asleep.

I lay there in the quiet and calm, enjoying the sensation of providing such comfort for another living being. Never had I imagined the peace it would also bring me. At least for now. There was a rough road ahead yet and I'd need to stay vigilant to make sure the beautiful woman I was already beginning to care about didn't come to any harm. A soon-to-be vampire and a werewolf prince.

Be warned, Dante, this can never be. They'll tear us apart if word gets out.

Chapter Seven

Amara

I came back to consciousness with an excessively harsh re-entry, my head feeling like it was about to explode. Then I realized I had company. Dante was firmly attached to me, his arms holding me close to his warm, well, *hot*, body.

Wow.

His being there was affecting me on an even deeper layer—damned if I wasn't horny, of all insane things. My mind shot back to all he had shared about my current predicament. How was it even possible in this day and age for such events to have occurred? A band of rogue psychos stalking the street looking for innocent victims? It boggled my brain.

He murmured something in his sleep, tugging me closer, his hand squeezing my breast and thumbing the nipple that stood at quick attention. *Oh*, that felt good, and best of all, the attention made me forget my headache. I rubbed my backside against his groin, and a substantial cock pressed into the crack of my ass. *Add well-endowed to his list of considerable assets.*

His talented fingers began to work my nipple, sending waves of pleasure directly to my throbbing pussy. It clenched almost painfully, wanting something to fill and satisfy its growing ache. Apparently, the world could be ending and a body still wanted what it wanted. I pressed myself against him like a kitty cat in heat, my other nipple begging for similar affection.

"You want it baby, say it. Speak dirty to me. Let me know how much you want—"

Nice. I'd always gotten off on dirty talk, especially when it was directed at me. Suddenly the delicious stream of sex talk halted as Dante came fully awake and took his divine fingers away, making me want to pout.

"I apologize. I must have fallen asleep." He sat up in bed, looking charming with the tousled thick waves disarmingly placed around his handsome face. He rubbed his jaw and all I could think of was that scruff teasing me between my thighs. I shook my head. What the hell had come over me? I'd been way too long without a man, was all I could come up with.

"No need." I kept my overheated face turned away. Thank goodness he wasn't aware of my raging hormones.

"Are you feeling better?"

"Except for the headache, but I think it's easing."

He laid a warm, broad palm on my forehead to check my temperature. "It's not scientific, but I believe your fever has lowered. The first wave must have passed."

"First wave?" Mystified, I sat up and looked him in the eye. He appeared amused by something that I was not party to—a roguish twinkle came and went before I could identify the source.

His expression grew serious. "There will be an escalation of the symptoms. It has to do with the rate of infection and its drive to overwhelm your immune system. You're strong—your immune response tells the tale. Some humans succumb to the infection in a matter of hours."

"Maybe I can fight this thing off?" His words had given me hope. Maybe I didn't have to change into a raving lunatic after all.

He shook his head. "Doesn't work that way, I'm sorry to tell you. Once you're infected, it will happen, no matter what. It's just a matter of time. The cocktail of drugs I prepared just eases the transition."

"To what? A damn monster! Then I might just as well end it now!" I was incensed that someone had done this to me without my consent or knowledge. "I can't live like that. Knowing I could attack another person? That's just not me. I've lived wanting to do better by this world, lessen my footprint or erase it as much as possible, not be a cause of bad things happening." I shook my head, tears held back by the thinnest thread.

He moved to embrace me, but I held myself off. What if I was to hurt him? The thought sickened my stomach. He didn't deserve that. Dante had rescued me for heaven's sake.

"It's not all bad. Not after you learn to control yourself."

I sensed he was still hedging, trying to appease me, not telling me all the truth. What exactly was this infection all about? And why me? The story about the movie star felt made up. Despair reached out a hand

and tried to grab a hold of me, but I fought it away with all I possessed. The sense of ants once more beginning to itch under my skin wasn't helping.

"I need you to tell me all the truth. The whole thing. What you've shared so far, it makes no sense." I shook my head in disbelief. "My whole world has been upended. Blown to dust in the wind. I have a damn right to know everything, no matter how bad it is."

His cheek twitched, a nerve jumping. "The world is not the place that humans believe it to be. At least, not most humans. There's an underworld. A world filled with supernatural creatures looking to live among you and make their way."

"What? That's—I don't know what that is!" A light bulb moment dawned. "You place yourself in that group. Not the human group?" *Crap.* Was I fantasizing about a guy who was off his rocker? Just when I was about ready to jump his hot bones…

He ran a hand through his hair, pushing the thick deep brown waves back into place. "I don't know any other way to explain this. Maybe it's best to show you."

"Show me what? Explain."

"It's a long story that began when Rome was founded. Long before you and I came to this crossroads."

"Rome, Italy? What does it have to do with this?"

"You know your history? About Romulus and Remus being raised by a she-wolf?"

"Yes. What about it?" Now we were going to revisit fairy tales?

"My family lineage was created at that time. Our DNA is different from most. We have unusual abilities. Physically stronger, the hearing and olfactory senses of a canine, extended visuals of a bird of prey and the ability to change our form."

"Change your form. What the hell! To what?" I rubbed my forehead, trying to keep up.

"This is going to be hard to grasp, but I need you to listen. Our genetic structure—my families and a few others—allows us to become altered at the sub-atomic level into pure energy. As energy cannot be destroyed, only altered, we can shift into a new form at this quantum level. It's like a frequency. You would see a sort of 'shimmering' during it. It's an all-spectrum-light-energy. It's not painful. One might just lose themself for a few seconds as their energy transferred from human to a new form."

"Okay, this is definitely TMI." I swallowed, my breathing becoming rapid. "Are you saying that's what's going to happen to me? That I will be able to shift to something else?"

"Not exactly the same."

"Fuck! Explain." My headache ratcheted up another huge crank of the torture wheel.

"You were bitten by a different species of supernatural creature."

"Right!" I reeled backward in the bed. "Pray tell, what kind?"

"A vampire."

The word hung between us. Just sat there before exploding like a shell thrown into a trench during warfare.

"And you're not one."

"No."

"Well, what the fuck are you?"

"A shifter, a werewolf of lineage going back to ancient Roman times."

"Of course, you are." I heard the hysteria in my own voice loud and clear. I jumped out of bed, faced him down, uncaring of how wild I looked.

"I have to get out of here." I looked around frantically for my shoes. I'd left them there somewhere, right? Then I remembered losing them. Fuck it, I raced for the door. Before I got there, Dante had me in his arms in a blur of movement. I beat my fists against his rock-hard chest. "Let me go! I'm not a monster. I'm Amara St. Clair, and I have a friend, Shay Wilson, and she would bust your ass for lying to me like this. For trying to gaslight me. How the fuck can you think you're a wolf?"

I punctuated each sentence with blows that lessened in intensity when I realized I was losing the battle. *But I won't lose the war*, I promised myself.

"I don't think it. I know it."

"Prove it."

"You're obviously not ready."

"Right! Because you can't, because none of this is real." I stopped fighting, trying to convince myself I was going to wake up from the nightmare. *Any second now…*

He dropped his chin on my head, pulling me in tighter, as if he wanted to protect me and persuade me in equal measure. "I'm afraid, Amara, that this is all too real."

His quiet tone of voice rang with sincerity, convincing me that at least he believed it to be true, that he wasn't trying to throw me under a bus. Or more likely into a dark dungeon. *Most castles have them, right, and this place was more like a castle than a house? Maybe I should be grateful he could never prove he was a wolf?* The very idea was disconcerting. *Sure, it's fun to read about vampires and werewolves, but have them spring to life in front of you? Not so much.*

"Is that everything now? No other dark secrets lurking in the closet?" I tried a lighter tone, hoping to catch him off guard, planning to run when I got the chance. The last thing I wanted was to be a heroine in my own life considered 'too stupid to live'. I wasn't born to be the sacrificial lamb. Blast it, now I was falling behind in my tight work schedule.

"Well, I think I've shared enough for now. Feeling better?" he asked.

"Sure, right as rain."

He frowned, but let me go.

"I have work due that I need to get done asap. And my computer is sitting idle back at my apartment."

"I'll have it brought to you as well."

"Must be nice to have all these invisible elves at your beck and call," I said as cheerily as possible, going along with the fairy tale while backing away from Dante.

I mean, the guy thought he was a wolf. Sure, I would understand having a wolf as your spirit animal, but to turn into one? At least that could never happen. Which meant I was back to being infected with a virus with no clear picture of what was going to happen to me.

Chapter Eight

Dante

How can I tell her that it gets worse, far worse than my just being a wolf? That vampires and werewolves are eternal enemies, and if she were found here, in my company, all hell would break loose? I need to take this more seriously, prepare the safe room as a last resort.

Even the extra fortification built into the walls suddenly didn't feel like enough, not when I had such an incredible woman to protect. I pulled out my phone and texted my assistant, letting Lenore know to pick up the laptop as well.

"Anything else you need?" I asked, glancing up from the phone to note that Amara was peering at me like I was a ticking bomb. Yes, I'd have to give her time to adjust to the new knowledge. Humans were considered an adaptable species, but this new information had to be beyond her ken.

Funnily enough, in centuries past it would have been far easier to persuade a human of otherworldly creatures living among them. Superstitions definitely had their place, keeping humans who believed in the creatures that came in the night safe from harm. Now, even though more had been written about vampires than ever before, no one believed. A loss really, as the world was far richer with the knowledge that there was far more to it than met the eye.

Hmm, Einstein had it right, in more ways than one, when he wrote about the most beautiful experience being the mysterious. It was what kept me glued to my microscope, hoping to use that spark to find scientific discoveries that would reveal and aid the world.

"Some of my clothes would be nice and my toiletries. And Rainbow's treats, his favorite blankie..."

I tore myself away from such thoughts as Amara began to tick things off on her fingers. I quickly texted Lenore to box it and bring it all. There was an upside — my assistant would be kept busy the rest of the day.

"How are you feeling?"

Her face had become more flushed in the last few seconds and sweat had popped out on her smooth forehead. My hand itched to push the soft strands away from her face, bend her backward and take one of her perky nipples into my mouth and —

Startled, I nearly dropped the phone, with only my lightning-quick reflexes allowing me to keep a grip on it. I knew what was at fault. Her sweet flower-like fragrance with overtones of human female in her preovulatory period or estrus was acting as a constant source of arousal for my wolf. And, admittedly, me. I might need a breathing apparatus that filtered out her incredible scent. Fuck, why did she have to be in the most vexing part of her menstrual cycle now of all times?

"I think I need to sit down." She swayed on her feet.

I moved swiftly to keep her from falling, sweeping her up in my arms and carrying her back to bed. Laying her down, I looked into her eyes. Her feverish look concerned me, clenching my stomach into a fist.

"I think you need another dose of medicine."

She waved me away. "No, no drugs. I need to sleep." She turned away, her eyes clouding over and closing.

I wished to know exactly the prescribed protocol of what to do for her. How to make her feel better. The unrelatable sensation annoyed me. I always knew what to do, priding myself on staying analytical and making sound choices. Why didn't I know the right thing this time when it most mattered? Most mattered? How quickly I'd been pulled into Amara's life and perilous situation blindsided me, something unscientific upsetting the natural order of things.

But as much as I told myself that this had to end soon, that I was required to report the situation to my family, I hesitated. Amara had fallen into my care like fate had deemed it. And it had happened at my family's casino. Surely, I was doing what was right and proper, taking care of her until she transformed. But then what? There was no future for a werewolf and a vampire. Even if I asked her to stay, she'd soon be wanting to join her own kind. It was the way of it. I needed to guard myself better, to see things for what they were in reality. Not thoughts of things that could never be.

I pulled up a chair and sat down at her bedside. Far-too-delectable scent or not, I would watch over her, make certain of her safety. The hours passed while I waited, steeped in worry watching her toss and turn and cry out in her sleep as if all the demons of hell were at her heels. My heart squeezed for her pain more than once, and by the time dawn arrived, I had made a decision.

She stirred and I waited impatiently for her eyes to open. Had she turned? Though restless for the last hour, she had not appeared in as much distress as earlier.

Then her body began to vibrate. I leapt to her aid. Was she going to have convulsions again?

"Amara, can you hear me?"

She moaned, her body jerking up and down. "It burns! Please, stop it."

"I need to inject you again. Will you let me?"

"Do it!"

I quickly filled another syringe and got the medicine into her, proud that I had managed not to ogle her incredible body. Amara was beautiful, no denying that, but she was so much more than just a gorgeous face. She was obviously intelligent and cared about others…and I couldn't discount either how receptive she was to my touch. She intrigued me on so many levels and I would enjoy getting to know her better, once she recovered. I ignored what that would mean, her turning into a vampire, and instead concentrated on keeping her safe.

"Better?" I asked a few minutes later after taking her vitals. I jotted the readings down on my clipboard.

"I'm not a damn science experiment," she said, noting my actions.

I paused in my writing. "Never thought you were. The intel might aid someone else one day."

"Okay then." She sat up and peered at the bedside clock. It was now two in the afternoon. "Have you been here all this time?"

I nodded and set my notes aside. "I wanted to be close by if you needed me."

"Thanks. What's next on the agenda?" She favored me with a suspicious look.

"You don't need to worry that I would ever hurt you."

"Are you suggesting someone else will?"

Right, she picked up on everything. Normally, I liked that in someone. "I know it's all been a lot to take in. You must have so many questions —"

"Only one. When can I go home?"

"All your things are on the way here. My personal assistant is seeing to it."

"Are you keeping me prisoner?"

"No, of course not! I just want to see to your welfare while you deal with the virus. You're free to leave anytime. But it's not safe. Those vampires will be lurking, waiting for their chance."

"Right. Vampires." Her scoffing tone told the tale. She didn't believe me.

I sighed in frustration. "Are you up to a demonstration?"

"Yes." She frowned, her expression skeptical.

I understood her stance. What person of sound mind wanted there to be supernatural creatures lurking in the world?

"I'm going to show you something. You need to prepare yourself. It's going to be a lot to take in."

"You going to turn into a wolf?" She shook her head in disbelief. All she was missing was a childish eye roll.

"Yes. I promise, he won't hurt you."

"Right."

"Are you up to it? You need to be certain. Some people find it too much and end up with PTSD."

"I'm ready."

She did indeed look prepared, sitting up and leaning against the headboard, clear-eyed, endowing me with all her attention.

"I need to strip first."

Her eyes widened with the knowledge, her fragrance filling the air with wonder and tension. Yes, a filter mask might be useful.

I undid my shirt buttons, one at a time, to give her the opportunity to prepare. She licked her lips as I pulled my shirt away from my upper body, nearly my undoing because I wanted to pounce on her at that moment and suck that pretty little pink tongue into my mouth. Concentrate. Sure, I was blessed with the usual werewolf body structure, all lean muscle mass and hard abs, but the way she was staring at me riveted all my attention on her every reaction. Yes, her pupils had enlarged, the irises almost vanishing.

"You know, music wouldn't go amiss," she ventured, making me chuckle in disbelief. Add a good sense of humor to the mix.

Maybe I should be getting into it? I knew how to dance, thanks to my mother's tutelage, insisting that all males needed to step up their game where females were involved.

Inspired, I gave a rhythmic twist of my hips, enacting a move I'd watched in a movie. She smiled and it was game on. I would do anything to keep that look on her face.

A full thrust of my torso made her smile broader. Then I undid the button on my dress pants, the sound of the zipper that came next drawing her full attention to my crotch. I liked it, being admired. Until now I'd mostly ignored the physical sphere, keeping myself restrained. But this being admired by the tiny human was enticing, fun. And if it took her away from her troubles for even a few minutes, it was more than worth it.

Chapter Nine

Amara

Dante had my full attention. There was an even better body under all those clothes than I had envisioned. He made me thirsty, the way he swayed to some inner beat for just me. I had never wanted a man more. Here I was, sick with a virus of unknown origin and results, and all I wanted was to jump his indescribable sexy bones. Then I remembered he thought himself a wolf and the moment was nearly ruined.

I twitched, pushing back hard, wanting to hold on to this forever, to forget the past twenty-four hours and stay in the moment. I'd never get to experience this ever again. I wanted to clap, to cheer him on, but restrained myself with the realization of how surreal this all was. I still had some decorum, though by the slimmest margins.

He seemed to understand my dilemma, going at it with even more wild abandon, shaking his booty as if his life depended on it. His pants vanished, leaving him in tight underwear that left no doubt about his endowment. *Oh my, is it hot in here?* I swallowed hard, licking my lips at the visual treat. I should be recording this for future proof. No one would believe me otherwise.

"Are you ready?" he asked in a sing-song voice, his handsome face alight.

"Are you really going to try to turn into a wolf?" My heart dropped at his question, unable to imagine how such an amazing man could think such a thing was possible.

"I am. Please, don't be frightened." He stopped dancing, his expression beseeching me to understand.

"I can do it, if you can." If it helped him to think his turning into a wolf was possible, okay, I could support him, as insane as it all was.

Then it happened when his underwear hit the ground while I was busy ogling him, so fast and simultaneously that it took me a second to realize what was going on.

Strange refractions of light, then prism rays of blue and white shot outward as a small portal unveiled itself right before my disbelieving eyes, like the parting of a mist. The breach expanded, revealing a glimpse into another dimension. One that beckoned with a depth of mystery and intrigue that boggled my mind.

Then, in a blink of an eye Dante disappeared, only for something else to appear in his place. Something that should not have been there. A giant wolf, gray-colored with bright blue eyes. A beautiful creature with lush thick fur, obviously in its prime and smelling of fresh pine and mountain air. I reached out to stroke its incredible fur, wanting to see if it was as silky as it looked.

He came closer and my fingers intertwined in the thick strands of his coat. *Amazing.* My heart pounded in my ears. The wolf was so huge I could climb on its back and ride the wind. The idea energized me, thrilled me. What would that be like? To be able to race through the forest or over a snow-covered glen, the two of us in complete sync and far from the human world?

Such a proud noble wolf, magnificent. I must be having a hallucination, to think a wolf was actually in the room with me. But nothing about the creature frightened me. Quite the contrary, its beauty spoke to me on another level.

Then the reverse happened. A shimmer of light and Dante reappeared, naked and yummy as hell. He redressed while I sat frozen in place. Had that been some trick done with mirrors like magicians did in Vegas?

"You okay?" he asked, joining me on the bed.

I wiped the sweat from my eyes, not sure if the wolf or the sight of Dante naked had been the most shocking. Or maybe titillating was the right word?

I trembled at his touch when he reached out and pushed the hair back from my forehead. "Well, you are a man of your word. You did manage to create the appearance of turning into a wolf."

He chuckled. "There's more where that came from."

"But it wasn't a person who believed themselves a werewolf that bit me, right?" I still couldn't go at it directly.

"No, a vampire. Different species altogether." His eyes darkened at my question, smoldering with such intensity I wouldn't want to be the asshole that bit me right now if Dante could lay his hands on them.

"Can they shift into becoming wolves or something like that?" I couldn't believe I was asking such a question in the twenty-first century.

"Some ancient species can. Others can turn into mist."

"I always thought vampires were bats?"

"That's a myth."

"Like all of this isn't?" I asked, wondering what bizarre universe I had faceplanted into. I didn't have the courage just yet to ask if I would have the ability at some point.

A growing sense of unease, of something crawling under my skin made me shudder.

"What is it?" His eyes locked with mine, and I saw the depth of his concern for the first time. The man was terrified for me. *Oh my God*, if Dante, a scientist, felt something really bad was amiss, I was headed for big trouble.

"Something weird is happening. I don't like it! Make it stop." I scratched and tore at my skin, the sensation an intense burning like a thousand hot pokers were scorching me from the inside out.

"It's okay, little one. I got you." He gathered me into his arms, pinning my hands down to keep me from digging holes into my flesh.

I thrashed about, heard someone screaming in horrible, indescribable pain, then Dante and the room vanished into a swirling whirlwind of darkness.

Chapter Ten

Dante

I rocked Amara in my arms as she lost consciousness, her pain mine. If only I could bear it for her, I would do so gladly. The tiny human did not deserve any of this. She was a creature of the light, a warm human being who should have lived her lifetime not knowing any of this.

My phone dinged, alerting me to a text message. I carefully lay Amara down against the stack of pillows and tucked the covers around her now still body. The final time was upon her and the outcome was extremely uncertain. Never had I felt such helplessness in the face of adversity. Science could only go so far in aiding her transition. Now she was on her own, stuck between this world and the next. Would her body be able to handle the monumental changes it was about to undergo?

Most didn't, a stark reminder that only added to his growing despair.

I picked up the phone to check the message. My assistant was back with Amara's possessions, and I could at least see to it that her parrot was well taken care of. I texted her back with specific instructions then settled down to wait, lying by Amara's side. The next few hours would tell the tale. Either she would transform or — I couldn't bring myself to even think of the alternative. I would stay with her, make her come back to me.

A knock on the door instantly followed by Lenore's voice asking if I was in there made me want to pound something. Hard.

I leapt off the bed, opened the door and stepped into the hallway, immediately closing the door so that Lenore could not see inside.

"What is it?" I demanded, unable to keep the impatience out of my tone.

"I was just checking to see if your guest needed anything?" Lenore said, her tone smooth as honey. Something about her demeanor bothered me, but I had little time to dance through the hoops to discover what my errant employee was up to.

"We're fine. Amara just requires peace and quiet."

"Is she ill? Does she have COVID?" Lenore's eyes rounded with her inquiry.

"No, nothing like that. Just needs to rest after an accident."

"Car accident?" she pressed, making him want to tear my own hair out. "Does she require a doctor?"

"No, just a simple fall. A sprain, nothing more."

"Do you need ice, a hot pack, a tensor bandage?"

What was she now? A fucking nurse's aide? "No. We're fine. Now, if there's nothing else—"

"I heard tell of a human being bitten while I was in Vegas with Andrew. Terrible thing, and happened right out front of your casino." She glanced at me with a strange look in her eyes.

"I know nothing of it. I'm sure my family can handle it."

"Yes, I'm sure they can. Well, if you need me for anything, I will be in the lab helping."

"No, I need you to set all the things you brought back from Vegas up in the room next door."

"But that's your room!"

Lenore appeared scandalized. What business was it of hers?"

"I want to see them protected firsthand. Amara's my guest."

"The parrot too?"

"Yes, everything."

"He's a noisy one. You sure about that? I could take him in for you. See to him while you're busy?" She licked her lips like the cat that had dived into a vat of cream. Not sexy at all. How had I been attracted to her in the first place? No, there had never been any real attraction between us, just a contract.

"Please see to it that I am not interrupted anymore today by anyone." Sometimes a man had to be blunt.

She nodded, her eyes alone expressing her anger. *Great.* Now I had a new enemy. At least she didn't appear to be the type to harbor a grudge.

I waited until she was safely down the hall before re-entering the suite. I didn't need Lenore to know I was harboring the very woman who had been bitten last night outside the Glitter Palace. The supernatural community was small and in no time my family would be knocking at my door, demanding I toss her out. Never would that be allowed to happen, much as I didn't want a rift in my family.

I hurried back to Amara's bedside, my worry turning to terror as I noted her paleness, her blue-cold skin and her slow breathing barely detectable under the bed covers. Grasping her chilled hands in my own, I wished my warmth into her. If only I could be certain that she would be okay, I could handle her being a vampire. I sent my prayer into the universe, *I promise to accept her no matter what, if you'll just let her live.*

The long tedious hours crept by, one tick of the second hand at a time. I lay down beside her, unable to do much but gather her into my arms and wait for her to return to me. "You must come back, Amara, I'm here for you," I whispered. I pressed a kiss to her cold lips, not mindful of what any other werewolf would think if they saw me. Amara needed me and that mattered far more. A strange sound, a high-pitched vibration under the mansion, forced its way past the worry. What the hell was that? Then I knew and the race to protect Amara from outside forces began.

I hit the alarm app on my phone. The entire mansion began to resound with the offbeats of loud, slamming noise, alerting everyone to a breach. Tearing out of the room, I raced for the elevator that ended in the catacombs far below the property.

Marshall Landon, head of security, met me halfway, his expression grim. "I've enacted the pressure switches. No way anyone's getting past that air lock, not without our knowledge," he half-yelled. "And if they do, I'll incinerate with all due prejudice and send those bloodsuckers straight to hell where they belong."

"Good." I nodded, noting Marshall was dressed for going out, not his usual uniform of all black. "I appreciate your staying to deal with this on your evening off."

"No problem, boss. Any idea who it is?" Marshall asked, his expression intense.

It was his job to get to the bottom of every security concern. He had to be told who was behind the attack, much as I'd prefer not to. The vampire I was about to mention by name had the worst reputation of all of them, and that was saying something, considering what the species had inflicted on unsuspecting innocents over the millennia. Of course, an occasional werewolf Nomad running rogue made my own affiliations difficult enough to handle. Even my pack being as rich as it got and having the funds to pay off just about any misdeed didn't make it any less morally reprehensible.

"Akar."

"Not the ancient asshole who was behind the assassination of the president over losing his hoped-for bride? Marilyn Monroe, right? And if I know my history, it was because he was convinced *she* was the reincarnation of Guinevere of Camelot. Another doomed love triangle." Marshall whistled. "One evil bastard. Why is he bothering us?"

I trusted Marshall. The huge, burly werewolf had been an excellent employee for eight years, one who kept his team in line. The problem was that if he learned there was a soon-to-be vampire hidden on the premises, I had no idea how he'd react. This was not the time for explanations. I needed to get back to Amara and make certain she was safe.

"Who the hell knows. The guy's already proved more than once he's not to be trusted," I replied.

While we shouted at each other over the ear-piercing sounds of the alarm, we continued downward in the elevator, both of us needing to see firsthand that the safety features were holding. With vampires able to turn into mist energy far longer than Lycans, who only remained in a state of energy exchange long enough to shift from one form to another, they were the hardest creatures to keep out.

An airlock should hold them off. But what if they hung around, waited for the chance to come in when one of my employees was arriving or leaving from work? That would make us vulnerable to attack. I needed to shut things down now, barricade the hatches. I had to make sure she was safe, do all in my power to make it happen.

Chapter Eleven

Amara

Dark, so dark. Had I gone blind? And why was I so cold? Like I was encased in a huge block of ice, or buried in a cave. But I couldn't move a muscle and that was the most terrifying thing of all.

Then the dark cloud lifted to a semi-twilight as my eyes adjusted and the hardness beneath me made sense, as I stared upward at a rough rocklike ceiling. Indistinct voices melded together all around me, murmurings just beyond my understanding. This was a dream, right? But it was terrifyingly real, like I had been transported somewhere underground.

I tried to move my head to peer around, but something held me in place. Why was I dreaming of such a horrible place? It had to be the trauma of the events in Vegas and Dante's story. The horrible pain had vanished, though I wasn't certain if this was any better, this creeping paralysis that froze me to the bone.

My heart chilled further with the rustlings of creatures coming closer to where I lay helpless to move or save myself. I'd never wanted to be in movies, and least of all, in a horror movie where the heroine is tied to the railway tracks. I tried to focus on that image, instead of how terrifying my current situation was, imagining breaking the bonds that held me fast, but nothing happened. *Right.* Now I didn't even have control of my damn dreams.

"She is so beautiful. Just like her. She needs to be watched over, protected, brought into the fold when the time is right. Until then, we wait. Soon she will be ours."

Crap. What a load of nonsense. *Please, please, let me wake up.* I dug down deeper, trying to find the power to break the spell of the nightmare. The struggle sickened me, my body warring within itself as I tried forcing myself to break free of whatever was holding me in a straitjacket, telling myself I had to do this.

I really couldn't take much more of this insaneness. I wanted to get back to my life, even if it was so ordinary that some people would scoff. It sure beat the hell out of this experience. My nice snug little apartment was looking better and better. I missed Shay and Rainbow more by the minute.

I had to try harder, *harder*. My very bones began to dissolve and I was losing the fight. Was I transforming, like Dante had suggested? The memory of the pain before I fell asleep rose front and center. Waking up might suck, but it beat this all to hell. Pain I could handle, the unknown not so much.

Push the darkness away, Amara. Come back to me. Be with me.

A swirling vortex blessed me with equal parts nausea and dizziness before I felt myself breaking away. Then the cave vanished and I was once again lying in bed, Dante holding me secure in his strong arms.

"You made it, little one," he said, tenderness lining his tone. "How are you feeling? Any pain?"

"No, no pain." I shook my head in disbelief though grateful for finally getting over the virus. I looked around, not recognizing where I was. The room was smaller and less lavish, containing the basics including a small office area with desk, chair and shelving near the bed.

"Where are we?"

"I had to move you to a safer location. While you were out, the mansion came under attack."

"Oh my God! Are you okay?" I looked him over carefully.

"I'm fine. Just grateful you made it through."

"My fever must have broken. The virus is gone, right?" I looked into his eyes for confirmation.

"The worst is behind you," he said, but I sensed a lot left unsaid.

"How long was I out?"

"It's Monday night, just after sunset."

"I lost all of Sunday and nearly all of today! I have work due Tuesday. I need to shower and get at it."

"I wouldn't be too worried about that. Your old life, I'm sorry to say, is over. You won't be able to do certain things now, to go freely in the human world during daylight hours."

"What are you talking about? I'm fine. I've overcome the virus and I'm obviously not a vampire!" If I was, I'd know it. In point of fact, I'd never felt better, like I could take on the world. "Am I still contagious?"

"Hmm, well, you did try to bite me already." A half-smile softened his words and lit up his handsome face, even as he avoided my question.

"You're joking, right?" I wasn't sure if I should run screaming from the room or laugh.

"Yes, you're fine. I've already prepared a special drink for you. Are you thirsty yet?"

"Some bottled water would be great." I was staying away from anything that could be tampered with, even if I did sense I could trust Dante. He had seen me through a severe illness, staying at my bedside, judging by the state of him, his rumpled clothes and a longer scruff of beard endearing him to me.

He looked just as great though, with the tousled waves of hair that curled over his forehead making my fingers itch. His handsomeness was almost a virus all on its own, making me want to nip and suck my way… *Whoa, make that I'm a* whole *lot better.*

He got up from the bed to respond to my request and he moved with such power and grace that it left me all too aware of how attracted I was to him….as soon as our paths had crossed, if I was being honest. "I had a terrible nightmare while I was sleeping."

"More like unconscious. I couldn't wake you since yesterday afternoon." He ran his hand through his hair. "I was going a little out of my mind with worry."

The sentiment was sweet, but I thought he might be exaggerating, considering my current rush of good health. "Really? I was that sick? I probably should have gone to the hospital."

"They couldn't have done anything for you. The illness is beyond their understanding. It was best you were right here with me. I know this virus better than most. I've studied it for over a decade."

A thought popped into my mind, now that I was safe on the other side. "What's the mortality rate?"

"More than ninety-five-point-six percent don't make it. I'm thankful that you're one of the rare lucky ones." His cheek twitched as he recited the harsh statistic — he'd been under more strain than I'd realized. Was he worried about getting sued? What I'd suffered had happened at his family's place of business, though the statistic he'd just relayed sounded like an exaggeration.

"I can't believe I'm still here. Maybe the RPS25 gene, the hallmark of ALS, or Lou Gehrig's disease, that I carry, had a hand in it? But no, that would be crazy. The gene is going to shorten my life, not help in any way."

His eyes widened as he handed me the bottled water. "You carry the genetic marker for ALS?"

"Yes. I've been tested, many times. It hasn't gone away," I said. I didn't mention that I also had early symptoms, the weakness in my legs that caused bursts of clumsiness being the worst one. The bouts of mental fog I'd just chalk up to exhaustion when I drove myself to work past my body's endurance. I had to make a living wage and editing took long hours.

"That is intriguing. Well, good news, you're cured now."

Anger and confusion fired through me at his blithely spoken words, followed by outrage. "Don't you dare say that! Promise me something that's impossible. Do you not understand that ALS has no cure?"

Taken aback, Dante didn't move, as I clambered off the bed and pointed my finger at him, my hand shaking from the upset. "Get out! This horrible disease took my mother. Don't do this to me. I won't stand for it!"

"Amara. Calm down. I meant you no harm." He held up his hands palms outward, his expression concerned. I hardened my heart. No, this had gotten too crazy. This was real life, not some goddamned fairy tale. I wasn't going to get any happy ending. Nature had seen to that when I was born. I had already lost so much that playing this kind of trick on me was a terrible betrayal that I couldn't—wouldn't—stand for. Playing at being a wolf, fine, but this, no. *Just no.*

"I don't believe you. Go, leave me alone."

"I'm telling you the truth. The vampire bite eradicates and cures all disease, protects each and every cell from dividing and aging."

I put my hands over my ears, in the age-old way to say, *shut the fuck up.* I also closed my eyes, unable to bear looking at him. Why was I attracted to a man who'd lost his damn marbles? I had to fight this attraction, tooth and nail if necessary.

"Okay, calm down, I'll go. But please, don't answer the door or let anyone else in here. There are outside forces looking to harm you, take you far away. I've also left a special concoction for you to drink in that thermos." He nodded at the silver canister standing on the night table. "Drink it when you feel the urge. And please, call me if you need me. I'm only a few seconds away."

I remained silent until he vacated the room. Then I screamed at the top of my lungs, uncaring if anyone heard me, letting all my frustration out. Calming down a few minutes later, I made a plan for the day, or should I say, night, remembering that it was after sunset.

It was a good thing I was feeling so invigorated. At least I could get some work done, spying my laptop waiting patiently for me on a shelf along with a new cell phone and a number of my things. A tiny stab of guilt hit me—at least he had tried to provide for me, watched over me while I was sick. But still, it didn't excuse his head games.

I found the bathroom and took care of the basics, not even bothering to check myself out in the mirror before pulling on a robe hanging behind the door. I threw my hair up into a towel and got down to work on the promised manuscript for my client. Halfway through the unedited pages, I jolted upright in the office chair. I had forgotten to call Shay. She had to be worried. Normally, after a night on the town we checked in with each other, and I had been incommunicado for two days! Unconscious, sure, but that was no excuse. I should have insisted on calling her earlier.

I picked up the new cell phone lying on the desk beside me and punched in her number from memory. That was something else I would one day lose the fight with as the disease progressed, something else I didn't want to think about. Then just before I hit Send, I paused. What was I going to say? I couldn't tell her the truth. All hell would break loose. Not that I wanted to lie to her, but why cause her more worry? Then the perfect solution came to me.

"Shay, it's me."

"Amara! Where are you? I've been trying to reach you. Are you okay?" Shay's frantic voice upped the guilt factor into the stratosphere.

"I'm fine. It's Rainbow. I had to take him to the vet and I stayed overnight with him. I'm sorry, I forgot to call you." I crossed my heart that I would never do this again. Lie to a good friend. But how in the hell was I supposed to explain my current circumstances when I couldn't even explain them to myself?

"Oh my God, Rainbow! Is he okay?"

"Yes, he's fine now, on the mend. Oh, and I'm not going to be home for a few days—the place is being fumigated." Sad to say this excuse rolled off my tongue.

"Not bed bugs again!"

I groaned in fake despair. "I know, second time since I moved in. No one seems to know where they're coming from."

"Great! Hey, why don't you come and stay with me? Save you a hotel bill. And your presence will bring the fairies out in full force, making my day brighter."

I almost panicked while I could hardly believe I was lying to my best friend. Fairies indeed. Shay had been the one who had seen me through more crises than I cared to admit to. And me with her if I was being honest, thinking of the late-night calls when she was going up the wall with worry over her dad.

"It's okay, I got paid extra for a project being in early and I could really use a few days of relax time. You understand, right? Plus, Rainbow will need all my attention. And you know your dad didn't take to him well last time."

A beat of silence. "All too true." Shay sighed. "Dad does not like his routine interrupted. Okay, I gotta run. Snavely's on the warpath. Again!" Shay worked for a trucking company, in the office, doing administrative tasks like signing off on loads hauled. John Snavely was the office manager, always going on about any trucker caught fudging their accounts, though it was a rare occurrence and easily handled.

"Catch you later, girlfriend!" Shay hung up and I sat back in relief. I had done the best I could. Soon, I could go home and everything would return to normal. Even as I thought the words, a part of me didn't believe them. An unease, fear of the unknown, was rising in me.

Nothing in my life had been the same since we'd won the contest.

A sharp pain twisted my guts and I rubbed my aching stomach. *Damn, I'm famished.* I glanced at the thermos Dante had left on the dresser. No, I wanted real food, not some crazy concoction.

But nothing presented itself and I didn't want to deal with Dante or anyone for that matter until I'd finished my work. Until I hit Send, I wasn't letting up. The thermos would have to do. I picked it up and shook it, making the contents slosh around. *Ugh.* A liquid breakfast was not my idea of a feast. I was more of a bacon and eggs with toast and jelly kind of girl.

Fortunately, when I unscrewed the lid and took a whiff, the fragrance was enticing, like a toss-up between peppermint and candyfloss. I poured a glassful, eyeing the thickish red liquid with suspicion. What was in it?

Drink it already so you can get back to work.

I took a hesitant sip as pain once more sharply gathered itself into a fist in my stomach. Then I was chugging the drink and going for more until the thermos was dry, my fingers catching the last drops. What the heck was in it? I wanted the recipe before I left here. My whole body was in orgasm, happy to be filled with whatever vitamins and herbs Dante had thoughtfully added to the elixir.

With the aid of whatever ingredients the drink contained, I was right back at work and finished the manuscript in record time. In fact, my fingers fairly flew across the keys, like they had a mind of their own. I checked the time—only five minutes since I drank from the thermos. What? That can't be right. I must have misread the time earlier. The work should have kept me occupied for hours.

But I was pleased anyway and sent it right off to my customer with the accompanying invoice. Now I could visit with Rainbow. I hurried across the room and twisted the doorknob, expecting it to open, but it wouldn't budge. I pushed against it, hard. Was it stuck? Awareness overcame me as new worry skittered across my nerves. I was locked in.

Stay calm, Amara. Dante did say that there had been a breach in security last night. This might be for my own good. Then why did it feel so terrifying?

"Dante!" I shouted. "Let me out. Now!"

He barged in, causing me to stumble backward. He looked frantic, like he'd been just standing outside my door, waiting for trouble.

"Oops, sorry." He reached out and, in a blur of movement, stopped me from toppling over. Of course, that brought me right up against the ridiculously attractive man whose fragrance was doing great things for my libido within a split-second of contact. I was way, way too attracted to this man. This crazy, insane, sexy-as-hell man who'd rescued me from a bunch of psychopaths.

"Are you okay?" he asked, like my answer really meant something to him. He did have a vulnerable side a woman could appreciate, under different circumstances.

"I'm fine, if I could just get out of here. I need to see Rainbow and get on with things." I tried to break free of him, but he was having none of it, holding on and observing me carefully.

"How are you feeling? Any cravings? Hunger?" he pressed.

"I drank all the drink you left and that seemed to take care of the problem." But even as I said the words, I felt a new hunger arise when I breathed in his essence. I pressed my face to his throat, convinced I could detect his life's blood seething just under the skin. I licked his warm flesh, wanting to taste him. Using my tongue, I traced a line along the side of his neck, pressing close to him, my nipples hardening with the rush of sensation. A gush of heat and wetness from my now wide-awake pussy accompanied the action.

"We need to talk," he said, pulling away and disappointing me. I wanted to stop talking already, just get onto experiencing this incredible rush. What was going on inside me? Who cared! *Just do me already.*

"Sit. I need to explain a few things about your condition." He gestured to a chair. I chose the bed instead, ready for what came after the silly lecture.

"Okay, Doc, let me have it," I said, adding a seductive smoldering glance for good measure. I had never appreciated how awesome my body was but now I ran my hand down one curvy hip that I showcased as I lay back on the covers.

Dante cleared his throat. The doctor had amazing self-control, I'd give him that. But I could break him, without a doubt. "The infection from the virus has made your body undergo certain changes."

"Like what?" I asked, watching him struggle to look only into my eyes.

"I know you don't want to hear this, and I apologize for upsetting you earlier, but you will stay forever young, as the song goes."

"Protection from aging? Well, that's one outcome that doesn't suck."

Of course I didn't believe him, but beggars couldn't be choosers and I did want to bed this big guy. He was a big catch. Tall and strong and powerful, I could only imagine harnessing all that male energy in bed.

"What about karma? Will I—you know—do bad things?" I just couldn't say 'turn into a monster and run amok'. Though the marvelous way I was feeling, I very much doubted that outcome. The memory of being attacked was fading, almost like it hadn't happened. Maybe because I was doing so well?

"Not if we treat this seriously. Keep you satiated and satisfied in every way."

I liked the sound of that before some misgivings crept in. I sensed I had undergone a metamorphosis while I had been unconscious and I was just now noticing the fallout. Seduction was normally not my game. I sat up and paid closer attention to his words, ignoring the lust for the moment.

"Oh crap. I'm not going to crave weird things now?"

"I know you don't believe me, but you are fundamentally changed. Have you noticed anything odd yet?"

"I may have lost track of time. I finished my work in what seemed like five minutes. Work that should have taken hours."

"That's fairly common. Speed, agility, mental ability, beauty, all will be enhanced. Of course, there are drawbacks."

"Beauty? I look the same!"

I remembered I had not glanced in a mirror when I showered, too consumed with needing to get to work. I slipped off the bed and hurried into the bathroom and pulled the towel off my head. A new and improved Amara stared back at me, one I scarcely recognized.

"Holy crap, I look good!" I ran a hand over my pale skin, perfect like marble, while my hair had never looked more luscious, undulating around my face in thick silvery waves. *Wait, I have dark hair. What the hell had happened?* I touched the new locks, feeling their weight and silkiness fall through my hands. They didn't feel dyed. The color made my blue eyes pop brighter still, almost a purplish pansy blue in contrast. This made no sense—what virus turned hair platinum overnight?

Were the myths and legends right, even though no one in the modern world believed them, well, except a few that needed their heads examined? Was I a vampire, doomed to need blood as part of my staple diet? *Never.* I'd fight that tooth and nail. No, none of this could be true. Until it was proven, no way would I believe. Someone, somewhere was playing a vast joke on yours truly. Maybe this was a daydream within a nightmare within a... Well, whatever it was, I was standing firm.

I stumbled out of the bathroom, dizzy with emotion. Dante stepped up and caught me.

"It's okay, we can fix your hair, though you are just as beautiful either way."

"What's happening to me?" My voice came out all thin and needy, not like me at all, though I did appreciate the vote of support.

"I know this is hard for you." He hugged me to his warm chest, offering reassurance in a situation that defied reason. To think I had not believed him before, screamed at him to leave me alone. Now he was the one here, offering help.

"As long as you drink the cocktail I will prepare regularly for you, you will find it within your capability to handle any cravings. Never go a day without it and you should be fine."

He raised his eyebrows at my look of skeptical concern. "You still don't believe me?"

"Well, I accept that you believe," I hedged, though the image in the mirror had pretty much convinced me, although I still prayed it was all a game of smoke and mirrors. The oscillating from belief to disbelief within me was the worst effect of all. I didn't know who or what to trust, not even sure of myself. "I get that you don't mean me any harm. Isn't that enough?"

He bit his lip, taking my attention. Such plush lips, so well formed like the rest of him like the earlier exercise had proven so well. I swallowed, wishing I could just lean in and kiss him already. If only we'd met under different circumstances. I reached out to touch his arm, not even realizing I was going to do it.

A pause, a suggestion of something important stirring in the universe, and his eyes flashed blue. A mesmerizing blue. He was going to kiss me. Of all times, this was going to happen now. Not on a romantic evening date in a fine restaurant, or out having fun at a ballgame with popcorn and hotdogs, but in some safe room hidden away in a castle in LA.

Then I didn't care as he pressed his lips to mine. The light touch of his warm flesh slipping against mine, his warm cinnamon breath, it all tugged at something deep inside, sparked an answering response, a match struck against flint that flamed to life. His arms came fast around me and I slipped into them like we'd been made for each other. He pressed against me and my body did all the work, shutting down my mind. I did believe that something well beyond my understanding was going on.

With increasing pressure, his insistent lips parted mine, his tongue in my mouth. He tasted and searched, devouring me. A swimming giddiness pushed me onward, and all restraint was lost as his huge body bore down on mine. We fell together in a tangle of limbs, hands busy trying to tear the other free of the annoying restraints of clothing. I burned for release, to feel Dante slide into my body, making me whole. I suddenly wanted it all, to be alive as I had never been before.

"No, little one. You're not in your right mind, I can't take advantage of you." He stilled, regret underlying his tone.

No fucking way. "I want this. My body — it's not my own, I need you to ground me. To make love to me like it's my last day on earth. After what I've been through, it may very well be."

He groaned as he absorbed my argument, like I was pushing him over the edge of reason. Good. I wanted this man, no matter how imperfect he was, for I was just as imperfect.

Chapter Twelve

Dante

Amara. I breathed in her heavenly essence. She wasn't making this easy for me. My mind reeled with the knowledge of how attracted I was to her, how I'd sat in the hallway with my back against her door so I could be with her immediately if she needed me when all I wanted to do was to shift and run for miles until some of the tension dropped away.

Her inner beauty and strong spirit, her intelligence and compassion, had all spoken to me on a cellular level during the past hours of her transformation, causing fundamental changes in me as well. She made me want to keep her protected and safe. *Forever.* The long hours of waiting for her to change had been indescribably painful. Had nearly broken me. Made me a different entity now. One that believed there was one special someone for everybody out there. The one-eighty shift in thinking was not scientific, not by a long shot, but it held a gem of truth that was blossoming by the hour.

To think she could have passed away at any moment in my arms, her physical body unable to handle the vast changes it had to endure. It had bonded me to her and now that realization terrified me even as it consumed my every thought and action. Forces were at work, all around us, and I had to hold my ground, stay strong to ensure she was given the choice of how she wanted to spend her life. If not here, with me — though the thought caused a rush of pain like no other — then somewhere else safe from that stalker Akar who wanted her only as a replacement.

"You're not yourself right now, little one. You've been through so much, more than any human should have to endure. If I could have saved you any of this, I would take your place in a heartbeat."

She stared at me in disbelief, her lips reddened from the kiss, her gorgeous eyes liquid with emotion. "But I've never felt better. And we're here right now, young and well, horny as all get out," she confessed, running her hands through her newly changed hair. It was an unusual side-effect, hair turning platinum, though not unheard of. The stress of the change to the body could cause any number of such things. A change in hair color was the least of them. Though I did miss the thick mass of dark hair, her new ones suited her well enough, though the resemblance to Guinevere and the movie star was more pronounced.

I looked away from her to make my thoughts clear. "You are under the sway of all the changes. You think you're in complete control, but you're not. Your senses are heightened, making the intensity of emotions far more profound than you will ever have experienced before."

"All I know is I want you to make love to me until the world disappears. I want to be unaware, caught up in the moment."

She reached out and stroked my stubbled cheek with her cool, elegant fingers, her eyes filled with an ancient wisdom that touched me on a fundamental level. The changes Amara had undergone were not just physical, but like an iceberg with eighty-nine percent of its vast bulk hidden under the water, so was her metamorphosis hidden under the surface of the womanly flesh. Flesh I wanted to embrace with every fiber of my being.

I took her hands between my far larger one, needing to convince her, though I was uncertain how long my chivalry was going to last just being in the same space with such temptation. "And I as well. But we should wait, until you are certain. Your emotions will level out in time and you'll feel more in control. It's a good thing."

Very old vampires often lose the intensity of emotions, leaning toward the true cold, unfeeling ones that everyone accused them of being. The thought bothered me more than I could say. When I was long gone, Amara would live on without me. The thought sliced through me, leaving me unhinged and making me want to head straight to the lab, figure out a definite way to live longer to be with her. Suddenly my current experiments had far more meaning, far beyond what I'd originally realized.

"I am certain." She amped up the intensity of the stare she directed at me, with laser sharpness. "I've never wanted a man more. I have a sense, a strange sense really, that we were meant to be at this juncture, you and I, that it's destiny. That we were chosen."

I swallowed. "That's a huge shift in thinking, Amara. You hardly know me, yet here you are professing such a thing. There's so much you don't know about this situation."

"Then teach me. Be my mentor. But that doesn't mean we can't be lovers as well."

Oh, the temptation to have her, to be with her. I was running out of arguments. And time.

I ran a finger down the cool perfection of her cheek, not bothered that her temperature had dropped a few degrees in the past hours. I was hot enough for both of us, always needing to run the air conditioner to stay comfortable in the lab.

"I want to teach you, little one, everything I know, but I want you to take it slow, be absolutely certain, because there's no going back. Our being together will just complicate things."

Surrender, my wolf commanded. *She's ours.*

Not that easy, wolf, I counterattacked. I had to stay strong, focused for the two of us. Or more like the three of us as I considered my wolf an entirely different creature, far more headstrong and volatile. At least that had been true in the past. Now, something was going on that defied reasoning.

"No," she said, shaking her head. "It will clarify things. I want to know all of you. The man who sat at my bedside and saw me through the worst sickness of my life without flinching and turning away. A man who thinks I'm beautiful even with this weird hair."

Her hand shook as she touched her head. It broke my heart.

I reached for her and held her tight, hearing my heart beat for both of us now that hers was stilled forever. She would have no idea of that yet, still caught up in the throes of change. But I could help her, see her through the difficult days ahead, give all I had to keep her on an even keel, even if my mission felt near impossible at this second. *A wolfman never gives a quarter, gives all to his mate.*

She wrapped her arms around me, closing her eyes and offering her lips for another kiss. My whole body trembled as I bent my head downward to capture their soft plushness with my own. The scent of her essence, a mixture of coconut shampoo and intoxicating musk that was hers and hers alone, filled me up like a run through the desert. Made my life make sense. I cupped one full breast as I kissed her long and hard, crushing her lips against my own and feeling her nipple harden with the slightest touch.

"So beautiful," I murmured. "You have much to teach me as well, Amara. How to be with you. How to be romantic and be a good partner."

"That would be my pleasure," she said, a warm smile lighting up her face.

She reached down with one hand and lightly ran her fingers over the prominent bulge in my pants. Her touch fired something stronger inside. I dimly heard my wolf howl before becoming frantic in my movements, tearing open her robe in efforts to feel more of her. I wanted to kiss every square inch of her, over and over again. My mind whirled with the intensity, the world dropping away to just the two of us. Her body next to mine.

I kissed and licked my way down her body between her breasts, the delectable taste of her thrumming through my bloodstream, making me want to devour her, hold on to her until the last day of judgment. Make her mine so that no other male would ever go near her. I wanted to drive away any and all competitors. Be there for her. Her best friend and lover. Her everything.

I parted her thighs and kissed my way from her calves to the apex of her thighs, pleased to see her pussy glistening with obvious interest. Parting the pink lips, I pressed forward to taste her, to savor the indescribable nectar that flowed from her. *Better than heaven and sweeter than the stars.*

I swiped my tongue the full length of her cleft, her moans of pleasure music to my ears. "You like that, little one," I whispered and she moaned all the louder.

"Don't stop! I'm almost there," she demanded, making me smile before I reapplied myself, sucking and tugging at her clit, thrusting my tongue deep into her channel. She screamed and grabbed my hair, her orgasm wild and free as she thrashed about, her body trembling with the intensity. *Nectar of the gods.*

"So amazing," she murmured as her body relaxed. She opened her eyes and looked into mine. I loved the shine visible in their depths, the sense that I could make this one woman happy. Very happy.

"Now you," she said, turning the tables on me. "I want to taste you."

She licked her lips and crawled on top of me, her naked breasts swaying back and forth with each tiny movement. I leaned forward, bound her long pale locks in one hand and tugged her pretty mouth toward me.

"You want a taste?" I asked, grabbing my cock with the other hand and guiding it toward her sweet lips. She nodded, staring with wide eyes at the length and girth of me. I thrust into her mouth, her lips parting before they closed over me, eliciting a moan. When her talented hands cupped my balls, it was all I could do not to come.

The head of my cock filled her mouth and I was careful not to overwhelm her, holding back. Her hands busy, I reached for a nipple, which jutted out, begging to be touched. I let her find her rhythm, let her stroke and nibble to her heart's content. She held me in her sway, a siren who spoke only to me, who only I could hear.

Reaching between her legs, I found her soaking wet again, her lips full and silky, her clit swollen and needy. I thrust two fingers into her, stretching her, preparing her for me. Her arousal had sharpened, nearly killing me with the instant need to possess her.

She couldn't hold back her moans as she milked the sensitive head of my cock with her mouth. I tightened my fingers in her hair again, directing her. But I wanted more. I wanted to sink into that sweet pink pussy of hers. I would brand her mine, make her want only me, the only one who would be able to satisfy her. I longed to stretch her until it was only me who could give her what she needed.

I pulled out of her mouth. "I want you. All of you."

I grabbed her hips and held her upward, straddling me. I teased her soaking wet lips and clit with the thick head of my cock, sliding back and forth down her swollen slit. Her breathing became ragged, her pale skin hot and flushed. She was more human than vampire, pulsating with need.

She reached down and positioned my cock between her legs. Heat pulsed as my essence slicked her entrance, the elixir guaranteeing her nerve endings would burn with a desperate need to be touched, to be rubbed against. Submissive, she had no control, had given it all over to me, her new alpha. In that moment I understood the power of sex, the drive to be with the one meant only for me. *Damn the science.* The sensations were like no other, each and every touch, taste and feeling beyond anything I could have imagined. This truth was the stuff of myth and legend.

When she whimpered, I pushed as far as I could into her in one long, satisfying stroke. Her walls surrounded me, tight and hot.

"So perfect," I murmured, losing myself for a moment in the sensation. She made me so thick, so huge. Then I began to thrust in time with her movements.

"Harder," she said.

I needed no other invitation, burying myself right to the hilt inside her, breaking through to the very core of her.

She screamed and scratched my back, digging her nails in as my cock tore through her, wanting to possess all of her.

"Are you okay?"

"I'm perfect too," she said, her voice low and throaty. I reached up and tugged on her nipples, making her squeal and push herself harder against me. Wetness flooded out of her and I wanted to lap it up. She smelled, felt and tasted of everything good in life. I rubbed myself harder against her clit, savoring the cream it brought.

I dimly remembered that I needed to keep myself in check or I would bite her, mark her mine, so every other male could smell my scent on her. I couldn't do that yet. Not until I had explained it to her, though every cell in my body screamed to finish it, desperate to experience the knotting with her, to swell fully inside her and bind her to me. *Make Amara mine.*

When the fireworks exploded inside my head and my release flooded my mate, we lay curled tight against each other. I drew up the covers to keep her warm, enjoying the way she trusted me to care for her.

"Rest now, little one," I whispered, but it was too late.

Amara was already sound asleep in my arms.

Chapter Thirteen

Amara

When I awoke sometime later, I discovered Dante's arms around me, holding me close. The moment was so wonderful, so peaceful, that I was reluctant to move a muscle. I wanted it to last, not be interrupted by the day's events that would surely get in the way of this feeling of everything being perfect, even if just for the moment.

Last night, our lovemaking had been a new experience for me. The few men I'd met never went downtown, preferring to have me do all the work then poking at me as if they were sharing the only part that mattered, their cock. Dante was different from any man I had met and gone to bed with, he shared himself, brought me to orgasm with his talented mouth and tongue and made me feel important. Like if I disappeared, he'd move heaven and earth to find me.

I was not sure how I knew that exactly, but it was a certainty. We'd shared more than just our bodies, we'd shared something far more vital, more generous, something I couldn't put words to just yet. Suffice to say he mattered to me now, on a primal level, and I wanted to see how it played out. I wasn't going anywhere for now. I wanted to get to know the man better. See him in his own element, maybe work alongside him in the lab? I dreamed of us being good partners in all things, discovering the other's strengths and weaknesses. It would take years, that was certain, for he was complicated. *A man for all seasons.*

"You're awake, little one," Dante murmured, his deep voice rumbling through me, eliciting a welcome response. I loved his voice.

"Just lying here thinking how nice this all is. Lying here with you." The one thing I was *not* going to think about was the changes I'd gone through. No. Instead, I wanted to savor this important moment and see where it took me — took us.

"Last night, it meant a lot to me," he said, his fingers toying with a lock of my hair. "So silky," he added. I refused to think about the new color, instead just snuggled in closer to him, pressing my butt against his cock that had gone fully erect in the past couple of seconds.

"Careful, woman, I'm about to burst again."

"Bring it on, tiger."

"Amara, there's something I should tell you. Being a werewolf, I have certain needs."

"Were they not all met last night?" I teased, thinking of the multiple times we'd made love. "I would think you would need sleep more than sex by now."

"Yes, the sex is amazing. Beyond my wildest dreams. But a male werewolf, when they take a mate, they mark them. The impulse is strong — so strong it's got me worried."

"What do you mean?" My heart raced at his words.

"I have to fight the impulse to mark you, make you mine in all ways."

My emotions settled down with his reassuring words. "I think I've already been well marked. I smell like you now."

"You do. And I of you. We need to shower again." His actions spoke differently as he rubbed his heavy cock against my backside once more.

"What is this marking all about?" I asked, curiosity getting the better of my commonsense. I couldn't see his face so I slipped around in his arms so I could read him better. He looked adorable this morning, his thick hair falling in waves around his face, his eyes shining with emotion.

"It's an ancient pact, where a wolf bites his mate to send his scent deep into her bloodstream to keep others away. It makes her unattractive to other males."

I startled when what he had stated so calmly sunk in. *"What?* Being bitten?" That bad idea brought me back to reality with a solid thud. "By you?" How could he suggest such a thing after what I had just been through?

I pushed him away, needing to get out of bed and get my stupid ass home.

"Amara, I'm sorry, I didn't mean to offend you. And I have no intention of doing it." He looked so boyish, his expression so concerned that I almost relented. I stood stiffly, my arms linked across my chest.

"What you just said, that was so wrong on so many levels. I was just bitten, for heaven's sake and it made me horribly ill. Now you're saying you want to do that too? Don't you see how crazy that sounds?"

"I know, I know. I didn't make up these rules. The marking and claiming has been around for centuries, since the building of Rome on the seven hills." He got to his feet and stood by the bed. "But what I'm trying to tell you is that I won't do it and I will fight the urge with all I have."

"No kidding you won't do it! I absolutely forbid it."

He nodded. "I understand. I won't bring it up again. I was just looking to protect you in the best way I know how by explaining it to you."

"Protect me, by biting me!"

He had no answer for that, just stood and looked properly chastised. I waited him out. I was not going to be the first one to speak. The seconds crawled by as we stared at each other across the room. He broke the silence first, taking a new direction.

"Please, I don't want this to change anything between us. Say you understand, that we can forget that I ever said anything about it? Start fresh."

I watched him for a few seconds, the space between us seeming to grow louder. God, he was crazy, but he was my crazy guy and I wanted to understand. But how?

He came closer, and I didn't back up. I probably should have, but his closeness drew me in. His vast charisma was like a damn magnet.

"I'm truly sorry if I upset you. I promise, it won't be mentioned again."

I drew a shuttering breath. "Okay. Let's shake on it." I stuck out my hand for some damn reason and he took it. He brought it to his warm lips and kissed each and every finger like they were the most amazing digits in the entire world. *See what I mean?*

He was my muse, my addiction, my sexual dynamite all rolled up into an incredible intoxicating bundle of man flesh. I could not let this powerful attraction go. I needed to be with him, discover why I felt this way, then spend the rest of my life writing about it when this surreal time period finished. *Because this has to end, right?*

It was a dream come true and it was a nightmare all on the same page. No way could I be on this kind of rollercoaster the rest of my life. It was too much. He was too much. But right now, I wasn't going anywhere. I would ride this whirlwind and damn the consequences.

"I would like to see Rainbow now," I said, pulling the shreds of my dignity around me like a cloak. Maybe what I really needed was a suit of armor with a built-in chastity guard? Did they even make them anymore? Then a thought burst forth that intrigued me so much I just had to suggest it.

"Any way we can go back to before this all started and begin again? Be two normal people that meet in some dorky cute way and laugh about it each time we see each other again? I'm all for being dared to approach a billionaire — you are one, right?"

He nodded, a slight frown marring his perfection, and I continued.

"And asking you for a date and you go along with it because your buddies egg you on, saying things like 'why don't you go out with a normal woman for a change, not an uptight scientist?'"

My little story almost brought tears to my eyes, the sense of what could have been under different circumstances. Not that he would have noticed me. Then I remembered seeing him while Shay and I were singing and he had looked very interested indeed.

"I'm sorry you and I came together under such dire circumstances. It's unfortunate, but it can't be changed. It is what it is."

"Well, that sucks." I frowned. "But you came into the casino the night Shay and I won the contest. What were you doing there?"

"You voice drew me in. You sing remarkably well." He smiled that devastating smile of his and his alone and I realized that was how we met. Our own origin 'meet cute' did indeed exist. Not in the horrible circumstances that occurred outside the casino later on and this was one I could live with.

"Shy and I love to sing," I said. "It makes the heart happy."

"Your singing can do that for others as well. I found I was really enjoying myself, which is not something that happens much in my world."

"So you're normally a stuffy scientist just pretending at riding a motorbike to elicit ogling sighs from women," I teased, liking the new footing we were establishing.

"I'm not pretending at anything at all," he said, a serious expression shutting down the moment of lightheartedness we'd managed. "What you see is what you get."

"I like very much what I see," I said, instinctively understanding that being honest was the only way to get his attention. He was indeed a serious scientist, one that searched out the truth and tried to make the world a better place than he found it. I thought about what he'd done for me, figured out a way to help me through my recent illness, a way that left most of me intact. My hair still bugged me, but a woman can't have everything.

"I would ask you in normal circumstances to visit the lab, see me at work and maybe even learn something of what I'm trying to accomplish here."

"Why can't I do that? What's stopping you from teaching me all about your work?"

I moved closer to him, loving the idea of learning from him. His great intellect was always on display, his eyes deep with mystery and understanding of things I could only dream of. Crazy aside, he intrigued me like no other man ever had.

"Your recent transformation for one. We're living in a houseful of werewolves that will find out in no time that you are different. And there is an ancient animosity between our species."

"Then take me away somewhere. You're rich—surely we can find a place where we can be together openly, work and be safe? Or we can go to my place back in Vegas. It's not much, but it's comfortable."

"There's no going back. I had all your things brought here by my assistant." Now he looked frustrated as all get out. "I can see that you don't believe all this. That you think you've only just recovered from a bad virus." He ran his hands through his hair, a tic beginning under this right eye. "I need to find a way to convince you, I can see that now. Seems the hair, the speed at which you can keyboard, nothing has convinced you."

"Well, there are tales of people's hair going white overnight. Marie Antoinette for one, right?"

"There are other symptoms lurking. For instance, you must drink that concoction I prepared or your thirst will overcome you, make you desire fresh blood. But I don't want you to experience such a thing so I can't deprive you. Maybe if you sit down and try to write a novel, you will see what I mean? Or try to run down some prey? Try to go out in the daylight? That will burn like hell, though, so I prefer you not try that."

"Okay, sorry I asked." But I liked the idea of writing a novel. The rest of his speech I was just going to ignore. "Okay, I'll try the test of producing a book. See how long it takes."

"That should keep you busy until sunrise, which is only an hour and ten minutes away. Then you will understand a bit more when you can't rise or make yourself get up."

"An hour to write a book?" I couldn't keep the skepticism from my tone. "If that was true, then wouldn't all the libraries be flooded with new books?"

"Most vampires don't write books. And most humans don't survive the change, as I explained."

I let out a deep breath. "Okay, I'll have at it. I'll give your words about my condition more credence if I can do this one thing."

"Data, creating and storing it, testing and proving a hypothesis with usage…that's a scientist's life's blood. I'll leave you alone for now. I need to check in with my people."

He came close and bussed my cheek with his warm, full, ever-so-tempting lips. And I certainly had the data to back up that assertion during this past number of hours. Now I didn't want him to leave, needing more of what had occurred between us earlier, another round of hot bedroom no-holds-barred sex.

"I want that too," he said, startling me. How had he known what I was thinking?

"But I need to see to things. I promise to be back shortly. Write your *War and Peace*. The world needs more such books."

"I was thinking along the lines of a sexy shifter novel with over-the-top action. I have way more data for that kind of story."

His eyebrows rose as a slow grin lit up his mug. "That will work splendidly as well. I just may need to read that one. In the name of science, of course. Make sure you disperse the data adequately, prove your theories."

"In the name of science, I may need more proof shortly," I flirted, gaining a wide enough grin to sink any thoughts of my wanting to leave here anytime soon. "Please don't lock the door. I'll latch it from the inside."

"Fine. Just be careful."

He took his leave and I took the world's fastest shower before sitting down at my laptop for the second time today. I made note of the time on the clock and jotted it down so there would be no mistaking it this time.

Hmm, what to write? Yes! *A Royal Bloodmoon Wedding.* An ancient celebration with the werewolf family coming together for a crowning of the new alpha couple. They were a royal pair, from the richest bloodlines, wanting the most magical, awesome wedding in the history of the world. I grinned. *My story, my rules.*

I loved happy-ever-after and royalty, with conflict occurring because the mothers of the betrothed pair were at war over every single detail, to the point the couple just wanted to elope. *But little does the groom know that the bride is on a course of revenge for a situation that developed between their families as teenagers and intends to dump his ass at the altar. Then a deadly earthquake shakes and rips through the town, separating the pair, making them desperate...*

The story flashed through my mind, with each scene creating an movie playing itself out in my head. I began to write, my fingers working in a blur of movement to keep up with the steady stream of words, paragraphs and chapters that assembled in front of my eyes.

I sighed at the lovely ending. The couple had come together after much soul-searching and painful, dark moments. I think I was in love with them at the end when they kissed while Vegas was burning like Pompeii around them.

There. Done. I figured hours or even days must have passed before I looked up again and checked the time.

Oh Christmas, only thirty-seven and a half minutes had passed? No freakin' way! I had the software check my grammar—maybe it was all just gibberish? But no, the manuscript appeared flawless at just over fifty thousand words. I sat stunned, thinking of the awesome ramifications. I could start my own publishing house, *House of Dreams*, fill it with books in a matter of days and earn a decent living by writing my own books. I felt the smile stretching the skin on my cheeks to maximum. My new reality had just checked in and it was not going to suck. Now I could only hope the virus didn't wear off.

Thoughts and ideas raced through my mind, landing on what had worried me for years, eaten away at my soul. Was Dante right? Did this also mean I was cured of ALS? I shook my head as if to clear it as a brisk knock came at the door. It must be Dante with Rainbow.

But it was not Dante who greeted me when I answered, but the woman from earlier.

"Hello, Amara."

I didn't like her tone or the look gleaming in her feral eyes that flashed intense blue even as I glanced at her. Why was she here? "Hello back," I said. I remembered Dante's warning not to open the door to anyone else. He didn't mean his own staff, surely? The woman had appeared a little too interested in her boss, so maybe that explained why we took an instant mutual dislike to each other.

"May I come in?" she asked, though the look in her eyes suggested she wasn't going to go away quietly into the night.

"I was just going to take a shower," I said, barring the doorway with my body. *Don't let her in.* The warning fired off in my brain. *Intuition is a good thing, it means pay attention.* Like the night I tried to avoid that asshole outside the casino. Of course, this brought all the bad memories back, making me want to run screaming into the woods again.

She sniffed the air deliberately, her nose wrinkling up like my fragrance was an abomination to her. Well, *duh*, I just said I needed to take a shower. "I was just checking if you needed anything?"

"No, I'm fine. Dante has made more than certain of that." Okay, I probably should not have said that last part, but she was all up in my face and annoying with her judgment.

"Well, if you need something, just give a shout." Her eyes narrowed, that flash of blue again, and she vanished, like a fart in the wind.

It was then another epiphany hit. I had powerful energy vibes flowing through my body, so invigorating I swore I could go right outside and cut enough firewood for an entire winter all by my lonesome. Rather unnecessary in the Vegas climate, but my Canadian relatives would appreciate it, I thought, remembering fondly the one summer I'd spent in Lake of the Woods and how I'd watched my uncle spend his time stockpiling the resource for the winter months.

Hmm. How strong am I? Maybe I needed more proof, more *data* like Dante had suggested?

Just let that creepy asshole try to attack me now. I'd whip his ass, I decided after finding it impossibly easy to lift the entire bed over my head.

Chapter Fourteen

Dante

I'd lost track of time, too busy with preparations. If we had to leave suddenly, I wanted a kit supplied with everything possible to keep Amara healthy. I refused to think about where all this was headed. My family would most likely disown me, once they heard about my connection to a vampire, or at the very least, do everything in their power to break us apart.

If only I could have gotten to Amara in time, before she was bitten. But fate, my nemesis in a world I wanted quantified and set up by specific rules that I could study and live by, chose differently. And damn it, I'd fallen for the woman as she lay in my bed dealing with the virus that seethed its terrible power through her fragile human system, tortured about finding someone to love and be loved by in a hard world.

I wanted to be the one she turned to, the one that no matter how difficult life became, be the one person she could count on to be there for her. She had no idea what awaited her. 'Vampires', for the lack of a better name, lived for the most part separately from the world. They converged in covens or groups with a common purpose much like Lycans who relied on each other for knowledge and understanding, though my family was prominent in the human community as well. It was the problem with sensitivity to sunlight that caused the separation for the species.

No doubt Amara and I would have to deal with the limitations and ramifications of her condition. But it could be handled. Who better than me who had studied the species?

Finally finished packing the medical box, I bore it on my shoulder and hiked up to the rooftop to store it away in the helicopter. I wanted to be ready to leave at a moment's notice. Hmm. The best location to squire her away to was one with fewer hours of sunlight. My family had recently bought an inn in the most northern outpost in Alaska that would suit. A place I could set up my lab and about the last place they'd look for us.

At least for now, until I could reassure Amara of the need to test her blood and design a cocktail that would help alleviate the daylight problem. No reason why one day she couldn't go about as normal, with proper medical intervention and care. I was also excited about what her blood would reveal. She'd survived when many had not. What made her different?

As I approached Amara's safe room, a series of tremors rising through the building caused my footing to falter. I leaned into the quake, struggling to hold myself upright. Was this it? The big one that LA was always predicting? No. I rejected that answer. Too coincidental. More likely Akar had struck again. Had he bombed the place? The bastard had gone well past narcissistic to downright insane. *Good way to draw unnecessary attention, asshole.* Unwanted attention was the nemesis for vampires.

Amara. I rushed down the corridor, intent on getting to her side. If that bastard harmed a hair on her head! I found her hovering inside the saferoom, her widened eyes telling the story. "What happened? Where's Rainbow?"

Damn, the parrot. No time to collect him. At least she was dressed now, fresh and clean from a shower by the scent of cleanliness that wafted from her body.

"He's safe. Best we leave him behind for now. We can come back later and get him." I cursed under my breath, prayed I wasn't lying. "We have to go. The building is under attack."

"Did you see them?"

"Don't have to. Let's go!" I put my arm around her shoulder and hustled her along, intent on getting her to the helicopter come hell or highwater. Where was Marshall? I pulled out my cell and made a quick call, holding the phone in one hand and Amara's arm in the other.

"Damn, no answer." This was bad. Was my head of security under attack? Hurt or dying? I had to get Amara to safety.

"Did you hear that?" she asked, her expression filled with dread.

"Hear what?"

She didn't answer but put her hands to her ears as if trying to drive something away, shaking her head as if in pain.

"What is it?"

She'd turned paler, her eyes even more frantic. She looked so beautiful, so fragile now as I felt the intense pressure of time slipping away. Better to just get her to go and ask later. I picked her up and began to run. My precious burden for once didn't question my resolve, just let me help her escape to the rooftop canopy that housed the helicopter.

"Buckle up. Cover yourself with a blanket. The sun will be unbearable otherwise."

Suddenly a number of vampires began racing across the rooftop toward us, streaming out and looking to surround the helicopter on all sides.

"She's ours!" Akar was taking point, leading a half-dozen dark and menacing male members of his evil coven across the confined space to confront me. "If you want to live, you'd better hand her over, dog."

Twenty feet and closing. No time for a discussion.

I leapt toward the metal box that housed the controls, my hands frantically feeling for purchase. If I could just reach the access electronic eye that raised the canopy, I could stun them by the sunlight that would pour in as the safety feature slid sideways and vanished into the rooftop. Fry their asses back to hell.

A shout of warning and Akar rushed to stop me. Straining with all my might, struggling to hit the switch, my fingers finally found purchase. A whirring sound erupted and the canopy was on the move!

The vampires stopped advancing, cringing as the rooftop flooded with direct sunlight. In seconds they vanished, back to the hellhole they'd come from.

I rushed to the helicopter, buckled in and started the rotors, following launch protocols in a flash of movement, then lifting the huge beast off the roof and directing it toward the north before I turned to check out how Amara was doing. She had taken my advice and covered up with the blanket.

"You okay under there?" I asked.

No answer. She'd fallen into a day coma, most likely. *Best thing.* I could get her safely to Alaska before the sun set and she rose again. I'd checked already on the status of the inn I intended us to stay at and it was empty of visitors. Just one person seeing that it was kept prepared for any member of the Luceres family on a moment's notice. I took a second to text Marshall, to see if everyone was safe. I hated to abandon my employees and my home of ten-plus years, but they would be well provided for while I was away. I'd make sure of that.

But right now, my only concern was Amara.

Chapter Fifteen

Amara

The voice.

It crept in, whispering in the dark. Of how important I was. And how much I would be treasured. It pressed into my mind, forcing a headache even as I willed it away.

"I made you. You who will be held above all others. Come to me and all will be well."

I hated the intrusion with every fiber of my being. The voice would not let up. Accusing Dante of vile things. Was this the creature who had bitten me? Or was I going insane?

"The shifter, Dante Luceres. He just wants you for what your blood can provide. Ask him this, is he not doing research on how to extend the lives of his own kind? He will use you. Siphon off your precious blood. That's the only reason he wants you. Not like I who will keep you safe from such things."

Over and over the information and taunts poured into my brain until I'd do anything to stop it.

"*Stop! What do you want of me?*" I finally cried out in desperation. Anything to make the voice go away.

"*Tell me where you are going.*"

"*I don't know,*" I answered in all honesty, grateful Dante hadn't shared the location. Betrayal of Dante was unthinkable. If I ever needed a brave heart, it was now. *Please, let me wake up.*

The weight of the universe seemed to be pressing down on me. If this was a side-effect of the virus, meaning this could happen any time I slept, I was in real trouble. No way in hell I could manage. *Wake the fuck up!* I screamed a million times, only to have nothing change. I was paralyzed, unable to move a muscle. *A living nightmare.*

Certain I was now a victim of PTSD, I found I could finally move my limbs a few hours later. I sat up in a headrush, but I was free of the voice. And Dante was looking at me with such affection and concern in his eyes I was overwhelmed for another reason.

"Are you okay?" he asked as he bestowed a sweet, warm kiss that stirred something deep inside me.

"Where am I?" I looked around, surprised to find myself in what appeared to be a motel suite. I was lying on the bed, covered by a lovely quilt that looked handmade by someone's grandma, with tiny stitches and colorful squares. The log cabin image was homey and brought a sweet rush of good feeling after the long, dark day of unholy rest that had just about driven me stark raving mad.

"Barrow, Alaska. The northernmost outpost in America. Also called Utqiagvik. A population of 4,927 at the 2020 census, up from 4,212 in 2010. It is the twelfth-most populated city in Alaska."

Trust him to want to share the data. It only endeared him to me more. I sat up and leaned against the nest of pillows, careful to keep the blankets tucked around my body. I had no desire to leave its cocooned warmth just yet.

"And what do the residents do for a living?" *Anything not to think of what had just occurred.*

"North Slope Borough is the city's primary employer. Tourism, oil field operations, government offices both state and federal, and of course, hunting and fishing. There's also a group for investment and development of the area set up by the traditional people themselves. But you're stalling, sweetheart. Are you okay? I've heard that the 'maker' of a vampire can contact them telepathically during their rest. Did that happen to you?"

I averted my eyes, not wanting to tell of the horror, but I did have one question. "Is there any way to stop it?"

"A blood transfusion might help. Dilute his control."

Suspicion rose immediately to the surface. Not that I didn't trust him—he'd been nothing but good to me so far—but it did raise a few concerns for me.

"Does that mean taking some of mine out first?" Did he want my blood after all? He was a scientist, looking to do research. Was that all I was to him? An interesting subject to study?

"That would be necessary, yes. Transfusion overload is unhealthy. It can cause shortness of breath and other problems."

"I think I'll pass. I'm queasy about needles and blood being taken." In reality, I was used to it, having needed to have many blood tests over the years. "What time is it?" I glanced around, looking for a clock.

"The sun just set a few minutes ago and won't rise for another twenty-two hours and eighteen minutes. It's November, the darkest month of all in Barrow. It's why I brought you here, so that you won't need to rest for long periods."

A rush of good feeling filled me. I threw my arms around Dante. "Thank you! That's the best news since this all happened."

"Of course, that means I can be a slave driver and get a lot of help from you in the lab I've already set up next door. We have the inn to ourselves." He added a charming grin to the mix, making me return the smile.

"I also want to write a ton of books!" My mind came fully alive again with the potential, last night's horror fading away. "I have big plans. I want to start House of Dreams, a publishing empire that I write a huge number of the books for to get it started, have other authors submit their work to. I want to mentor the writing community. I can make a living at it with the speed at which I can produce stories."

"That's about the most unique use of extraordinary speed that I've ever witnessed as an outcome of the virus. You are one in seven point nine billion, Amara St. Clair."

A rush of confidence filled every cell in my body. Yes, if I could stay here, away from the sun and not have long periods of rest, I could do okay. Maybe even flourish. Then my heart fell. What about Shay? She was so far away.

Dante must have observed my expression, because he put his arms around me for a hug, patting my back. "I know, it's rough at first. But I'm here for you. Always know that. I'm not going anywhere, ever. You have my total commitment."

I pulled away, uncertain of what to think of that. "I can't ask that of you. You have family, a home to return to, employees and valuable work to continue." Then I remembered the attack and how very much his life had been upset by what had happened to me. Things he would not have asked for and I wouldn't wish on my worst enemy.

"It will work itself out. Don't worry about me. I never do anything I don't want to. Ask anyone in my family, I'm the essential rebel. The one who can't live under their roof. That's why I was in LA, not Vegas like the rest of the pack. I can work here, in Alaska quite happily for weeks on end. Then we can move, follow the waning sun around the world. I have the resources to do that."

"You want to be with me that long?" The question popped out all on its own, unfiltered and blush-inducing.

"I do. I think we need to give this new thing between us some time. It's intense, the rush of being with you, but with more data, we'll know if we're the right one for the other. To discover whether our interests converge and if our personalities are compatible?"

I laughed so loud my belly hurt and tears rolled down my face.

"What's so funny?" His hurt, boyish expression calmed me down.

"Only you would see it that way. Needing more data. But you're not wrong. Time spent together would tell the tale, not that I'm saying that's going to happen for certain. I have a friend back in Vegas who will not understand my being away so long. What do I tell her?"

The idea of working with Dante did intrigue me. I was a sponge about learning new things, and having complete access to a previously unknown world did have enormous attraction. Plus, it would give me time to know if this was all real, or if I'd been thrust into some kind of bizarre universe that I needed to escape from, though I had no idea how at the moment or even if I wanted to.

"Shay, is it? Your friend?"

I nodded.

"Have you ever expressed a need to her for traveling abroad?"

"No, I've pretty much been a homebody. Work has consumed me."

His eyes lit up. "There. We have that in common."

"So, what do I do?"

While my mind worried over the problem, it occurred to me it was morning and I yet to feel the need to rush to the bathroom and take care of normal needs. What was up with that? Talking about needs, another one was stirring as I watched Dante mull over the problem. He was just so big, strong and handsome. I wanted to have that body mingling with mine, flesh on naked flesh. I reached out and tucked an errand curl behind his ear. He had gorgeous hair, thick and silky to the touch. I ran it through my fingers, lingering.

"How often do you normally see her?" he asked, not totally unaware of what I was thinking, judging by the look of keen interest that stirred in his dreamy brown eyes. He picked up my hand and kissed each finger, sending delicious tendrils of heat racing through me. Well, he knew me and what I liked in one important way.

"A couple of times a month, but we talk almost daily." I opened the buttons on his shirt and trailed one hand down his chest. It had just the right amount of springy hair and I enjoyed the taut muscles then the hardness of his erection that pushed at his pants, suggesting we were both on the exact same page.

"Talking's easy. She won't know where you are. And we can make arrangements to slip back into Vegas once a month or so. Keep her from being suspicious and keep your friendship alive, since it means so much to you. But you will have to be careful not to tell her anything about your new life."

"I don't want to be locked up for being a lunatic, so that will work. Now, let's forget the world for a while." I tugged at his belt, punctuating my remarks, my nipples hardening and begging for his full attention.

"Are you sure you're up for that? You just woke up after a hard day's night."

"Data says I'm absolutely one hundred percent positive."

His wicked grin said it all.

My panties flooded with wetness, my sex swollen and needy as I gazed at his heavy-lidded expression. I ached for him. So much power filled his hard body, more than I had ever experienced in a man before. But he was no ordinary man. I gave into him with pure pleasure, my body stronger at the moment than even my newly awoken mind, for I could not have turned away from having this man if my mortal soul had depended on it.

He kissed me, soft at first, then with an intensity that rocked me. His mouth devoured me. I moaned, wanting him more than I could say.

He tore off the covers with impatient hands, pulled up my night gown and applied his mouth, tightening his lips around a budded nipple. He licked around the sensitive peak, then suddenly drew hard on the vulnerable tip, making me vibrate with need.

"I want to taste you. All of you," he breathed against my breasts. Then he reached down with hands that demanded I submit to his will, and pulled down my panties. When my underwear was free, he raised them to his nose and breathed deeply. He shrugged off his pants, blessing me with the spectacular view.

"You smell like sex and honey." In a flash, he flipped me so that my legs were braced on either side of his body, revealing my mound to his view. I let my legs fall farther apart. I wanted him to see me. To see how wet I was for him.

"Perfection." He gazed hungrily at my nakedness before he dipped a finger between my folds and found my clit. He massaged it in tantalizing circular motions, the expert caresses making me moan, unable to deny how turned on I was. When he applied his mouth to my core, the nerve endings tingled and sprang to life, vibrating as I was thrust into a world of pure sensation. A world which was all about gratification and desire. I couldn't think. My clit was swollen and aching and my thighs slickened with the fluid that spilled from me.

He lapped it up, sweeping his raspy tongue along my inner lips, dipping into my channel and licking deep within me. Using his talented hands against clenched tissue, he stroked, working his fingers inside me as violent pleasure lashed me. All the while he sucked and nipped at my clit. It was too much. I went to push him away, but he continued, overriding my weak objections.

"Come for me."

His commanding tone pushed me to the edge. I opened to him, let him feel all my pent-up desire. And when I could not take any more of his probing fingers stretching and rubbing against and in me, the throbbing increased to a crescendo and I spiraled into the abyss, falling completely apart.

I opened my eyes in wonder sometime later, too satiated to move for the moment.

He smiled down at me as I still lay sprawled before him, unashamed in all my glory, a wide, wolfish smile that made my heart lose a full beat. I glanced down at the apex of his strong thighs, where his cock stood at full attention, begging to be kissed.

I smiled back. "My turn."

I took my time, licking and teasing all along the long thick length of him. He had a beautiful cock, strong as steel and velvety smooth at the same time. I eased him into my mouth, enjoying the sensation of control as he moaned with each stroke of him, applying suction to push him toward the edge of no holds barred.

He stopped me then, pulling my head back as he fisted my hair. "No, I want to be inside you." His low growly voice turned me on even more, vibrating through my core.

"Yes." That was all I could manage before he was centered between my thighs and pushing himself inside me in one powerful action that took my breath away. He was so large, so much, that I had to soften to allow him to seat himself fully. But once he did, he was pounding into me like the world was going to end today. And what if it did? I would die in the throes of the greatest passion. One I had no idea existed. I was becoming addicted to sex with Dante after such a short time—he was my crack cocaine, and there was no holding back. We gave each other all we had and it still wasn't enough. Twenty minutes later we were at it again. Time passed in a swirl of sexual energy and acute desire until the room was scented with our mingled fragrance.

Many, many hours later we finally fell into a deep sleep after I drank deeply from the thermos of essential ingredients, one he'd retrieved from one of the bags he'd brought along. Then Dante and I curled tight around each other. In Dante's arms, the voice softened in intensity in my head, giving me needed respite.

Chapter Sixteen

Dante

When I woke up, Amara was still fast asleep in my arms. My wolf needed to run, have the space to make sense of all the recent changes. *Fate.* Was the entity I'd always denied entering my life now of all times and making me change my whole perspective on who I was and how the universe operated?

I'd always considered fate equivalent to being pushed around by an omnipotent entity or by psychologically predetermined behavior or by mechanistic socioeconomic forces, thinking I flew above it all. That self-determination was my birthright. Was I predestined to be with someone? Amara St. Clair had taken over my every thought since she'd been thrust into my sphere of influence, an unheard-of situation for a wolfman consumed with the scientific side of things.

Never had I imagined being at such a crossroads. Much as my intellect wanted to reject the premise, my body and heart were sending different signals. Lying beside Amara, breathing in her essence, just felt so damn right. *Predestined.*

I slipped out of bed naked and closed the door to the suite softly, wanting Amara to get all the rest she required. Down the wide staircase I rushed, desperate for fresh air and wide-open spaces. Soon as I reached the edge of the small town, careful to avoid any humans, I shifted, leaving the present dimension for the one on the other side of the membrane. The thick fur was an instant warmth against the deep freeze of the far northern region in the dead of winter.

I sniffed the frigid air with interest to read the signals, my breath a frost haze about my face, catching the scent of other predators on the stiff breeze. *Polar bear and white wolf.* Neither worried me. I'm a gray. The strongest, swiftest, most powerful predator of all. It would take ten cold ones to bring me down, and even then, the outcome was not certain.

I ran for miles and miles, until nature's purity blew away any lingering doubt of my ability to think straight. Yes, fate had intervened in my life. Now, the options were limited. No longer did I just have myself to worry about, but the care and protection of another. The most precious one of all, Amara St. Clair. I accepted that the universe had chosen me for her, that some divinity had intervened. This was no dress rehearsal, but real life, one I needed to live up to. But how to make the perfect plan, based on proper data, when I didn't know the quantitative rules to apply?

I was so involved with unscrambling my thoughts that I nearly missed it. *Amara.* She was in pain, her mind and body under attack! I turned around and raced back toward the inn, angry for allowing myself to be so far away now when she needed me again.

When I got back, the dark had returned, meaning she could rise once more. I found her huddled under the quilt, her face bleak and pale, and when she saw me in the doorway, she jumped to her feet, racing to embrace me.

I held her trembling body, the worry taking hold of my mind with iron claws. "It's going to be okay, little one," I said, holding her close to my heart, sharing my warmth.

She shook like the last leaf attached to a tree by the slimmest of threads, ready to release at any moment and fall to the ground. Her body was ice-cold, her tone bleak when she answered me. "I don't know that it is, Dante. He came at me, tried to force his thoughts on me, press his body against mine in some kind of horrible, disgusting way. He wants me to betray you. I told him I would never do that and he said he will only increase the pain and apply more pressure. He promised me he will never, ever, let me go."

"It's okay. I can keep you safe." I stroked her hair. Why had I left her alone?

"I should go, I don't know where or how, but this is not fair to you. I can't be trusted. I know that now." Her bleak tone tore my heart in two.

"No, I won't allow that. We can do things. Try things. Move on to another location when we need to. Don't give up now." My resolve was unchanged by her confession. I could never let her leave to face it alone. Not unless there was no breath left in my dying body.

Her shoulders still slumped, she pulled away from me, her unfathomable pain shaking me to the core.

"I may bring more danger to you than we originally thought. He's insane, impossible to reason with."

"There are things we can try. Now. During daylight hours, we can do a blood transfusion. Possibly dilute his control."

"Your blood?"

"No, that's far too dangerous. Human blood is safer. I've stocked some in my medical bag in case of this eventuality."

"Okay, I'll try anything. Let's do it now."

"I'll be right back." I kissed the top of her head and hurried from the room, intent on collecting my medical kit left in one of the rooms for safe storage.

When I reentered Amara's suite, the shower was running and I went about setting up a makeshift hospital bed, attaching the IV line to a collapsible pole I assembled in record time.

Amara came into the room, hair wet and lying over a fluffy robe that the suite provided. She looked so young and beautiful, so vulnerable without a stitch of makeup on that my heart squeezed again just at the sight of her. Her eyes flickered to the setup I'd completed.

"Will you drain any of my blood first?" she asked, a frown knitting itself between her eyebrows. I wanted to reassure her, keep her demons at bay so badly that I could taste the desperation.

"No, not this time. If we need to do it again, I will have to. Lie down on the bed, please."

She did as I asked, arranging herself against a nest of pillows, her robe chastely tucked around her slim body. A body I adored and wanted to make my own as often as possible. My cock rose in agreement and I chastised myself for such thoughts when she was in a bad way.

"This will sting a bit, but I'll try to be gentle," I explained, picking up an alcohol swab and applying it to her arm before placing a needle into a prominent vein and taping it in place. I opened the special lock on the round plastic tube and the two of us watched the red liquid follow the curve from the IV bottle down to her inner elbow.

"How long does it take?" She grimaced as the blood began to enter her system.

"Not long." I lay down on the bed beside her, and held her free hand, pressing it against my heart while we waited.

"I can't imagine a pint or two of blood changing much," she said, her tone skeptical.

"It's a step in the right direction. And I won't leave you alone ever again while you rest. Can you forgive me?"

"What? There's nothing to forgive. You can't give your life up for me. That's unfair and I would never ask that of you. But I am curious… What did you do out in the freezing Arctic this morning?"

"I went for a run."

"In this bloody cold! I hope you bundled up warm?" She lay with her head against my chest now and the gesture was touching.

"Well, I was covered with a thick layer of fur."
Silence.

Then she asked quietly, her hand lying limp in mine. "This is all real, isn't it? I've fallen into the world of vampires and shifters, like in some novel. Are there any more surprises? Other creatures to watch out for?"

"Well, witches and warlocks, of course."

"Of course."

"And some countries have their own supernaturals, like the sasquatch and the kraken. Too many to mention really. I do have a complete list you're welcome to peruse."

"TMI. Maybe later. Though I am curious who's at the top of the pyramid?"

"Lycans of course, but in reality, it depends on who you ask. Most keep to the shadows. Humans are not known for tolerance around anything that looks or acts differently from them. And any super ability would make a target."

"But you live in plain view."

"Easier for us than others who can't live in sunlight or exposure due to their unusual form. Not to mention boatloads of money solves most anything. We are one of the three houses that split apart in the annals of history, House of Luceres, House of Anche and the infamous House of Ribelle. But we're the house that capitalized on every opportunity and became the most successful of all time. And who really believes we exist anyway? Right, time to deal with your apparatus." I noticed the blood supply in the plastic bag was running low and leapt off the bed to handle it.

Amara watched me remove the needle and place a cotton ball in her inner elbow with a piece of tape to cover it. "It will heal quickly. One of your superpowers I forgot to mention."

"That's something anyway." She shrugged. "You haven't taken any of my blood to test yet?"

"I didn't want to upset you." I could only imagine the lies Akar was filling her head with.

"No, it's fine. Take some and find out all you can, please. And I want to work with you on anything I can to help you. Maybe my blood will be useful in some way."

"It might have some answers for us. I'll do it now if you want?"

She nodded. I quickly did the deed and retaped her inner arm. "There. You need to have a drink now and a rest."

"I want to come with you. I'm not tired at all. Just let me get dressed."

"I'll meet you next door. You start removing articles of clothing and I won't be able to answer for myself."

She blessed me with a coy smile, and slowly lowered her robe revealing the curve of her rounded breast before dropping it lower and lower until she revealed all of herself.

Of course I was up to the challenge. As was my wolf.

Chapter Seventeen

Dante

"How did your family come to own an inn at the top of the world?" Amara looked up from the task I'd given her of setting up a sterile area.

"Long story." I was running tests on Amara's blood through the dexometer I'd invented to show the strands of DNA in far less than the normal time. We'd know her blood's components in mere minutes.

"We have time. I'd like to know. Strange place to find billionaires, I'm thinking."

"It's quite the tale. My cousins, Maximus and Alessandro, found their mate, Trinity, and brought her here."

"Wait! Two men, one woman? Is that common in your world?"

My wolf growled. "No. Very uncommon and due to the fact that the cousins are monozygotic twins. Don't even think about it."

"Not possessive at all, eh?" Amara teased, her smug smile telling the tale.

I kept myself in check by the narrowest of margins, recognizing jealousy for the confounding emotion it was and deciding wisely to continue the story. "They were looking for a very special artifact they'd been scouring the earth to find for a number of years."

"Did they find it here, in Alaska?" Amara stopped disinfecting a beaker to ask, her hand poised mid-air.

"They did and it saved their Forever Mate's life." An image of the Lupus Sanguis chalice rose in my mind. I'd tested it every which way from Sunday and was still confounded as to why it had worked. It might be made from the original blood and bone of the first wolf but it held its secrets close. I had been unable to recreate a successful experiment with its presence in my lab, try as I might. Something had been missing and damned if I knew what. If I was not a scientific wolf, I would have said *belief*. The placebo effect was what I had to chalk the whole thing up to in the end.

"Forever Mate?"

"The descendants of the original wolf, Houses Luceres, Anche and Ribelle, all have a belief in one perfect mate."

"And you don't?"

"I didn't give it much thought or credence until recently actually." I shrugged off her question. I just knew my attraction to Amara went further than I'd ever gone before. To think that destiny was playing a hand in it was causing me undue pain, considering how I'd lived my life to date, something I'd question for a long time to come. The beliefs and thoughts of a lifetime don't change overnight.

"How does the chalice work?" she asked.

"I wasn't there for the event, only tried to recreate it in the lab, unsuccessfully, I might add, but when their mate was bitten by a Nomad, a wolf broken away from a pack, they both gave their blood and she drank it, curing her of the terrible illness that nearly killed her."

Amara shuddered. "Blood again. What is it with this world and blood?"

"Blood is life. It contains all the mysteries of every species in the world ever born in a single drop."

"Do you think the chalice would help me?" She appeared pensive, deep in thought, when I flickered my eyes toward her.

"Don't even think about it. It's far too dangerous. It would mean me biting you"—I grimaced at the barbaric idea—"and doing some ancient voodoo to cure you."

"But maybe it would break his hold over me." Her eyes shone a little too bright for his liking.

"Or kill you. I can't have that." The thought about drove me to my knees and a glass vial slipped from my fingers and broke into shards on the tile floor. "Shit!" The expletive slipped out.

"I'm sorry. I didn't mean to upset you talking about it."

"I'm fine. Move away—I don't want you cutting yourself." I bent to the task of cleaning up the mess. Such a thing had rarely happened, I couldn't ever remember having an accident. I had lightning-quick reflexes.

I finished up and glanced at Amara. Oh no, tears glistened in the depths of her beautiful eyes, threatening to derail all my best intentions.

I rushed to take her in my arms, smoothing her hair back. "I'm sorry, I didn't mean to upset you. I'm afraid this thing has me more perturbed than I realized. I can't remember ever dropping anything while working on an experiment."

"It's me that should apologize. I've been a bit off since this whole thing came down."

"You? You've been amazing." I couldn't believe what she was saying. Amara was so strong. I'd watched her heroic recovery, thinking I was the one who needed to try harder to be worthy of her.

"I don't feel amazing. I feel like a bit of seaweed drifting on a vast ocean, not certain where I'm going to get tangled up or which shore I'll land on."

"I've got you. We can do this together." I needed to reassure Amara, keep her from ever doubting herself.

"Promise me, if nothing else works, and before I'm driven insane, you will share your blood with me? It might be the only thing to save me, crazy as it sounds. I believe we are here, at this juncture, for a reason. I know you don't believe in fate, but I do."

"I'm beginning to question all my beliefs, quite frankly. Now, dry your eyes, we have work to do."

"Promise me first that if I can't speak for myself, you will bite me."

She wouldn't let it go, that was obvious now. I was fairly certain it would never come to that. *Best to promise and alleviate her worry.*

"Okay, I promise. Now, work."

"Slave driver," she teased, but thankfully wiped her eyes and got back to her task.

"Oh, you have no idea, sweetheart, what I am capable of," I teased back, wiggling my brows at her to make her laugh. How I loved to hear her laugh.

Chapter Eighteen

Amara

A loud blast of something exploding nearby shook the very floor we were standing on.

"What's going on?" I asked, rushing to join Dante who had moved to the window, drawing back the drapes.

"Something exploded. Shit, right next door — the building's on fire! I need to go and help."

I had not met any of the neighbors in the scant twenty-four hours we'd been in Barrow. I'd been warned by Dante to keep a low profile and not draw any attention.

As the fire spread, I knew it was bad. In no time, the building would be gutted and they were only fifty feet away. What if the inn caught fire? What then?

"You stay here. I'll help put it out."

A banging on their suite door interrupted us.

"Go to the bedroom. I'll answer it."

I raced to do as he asked, not bothering to question what was an obvious directive. I had barely closed the bedroom door before I heard the person burst into the room, the door slamming in the process.

"You need to get out, Mr. Luceres, the propane canisters are about to explode."

The man's loud voice carried into the bedroom. I hated hiding away from the world, the fact driven home by the current dire circumstances. *Crap. Don't ever think things are fine because shit can happen in a split-second.*

"I'll be right down. I just need to gather a few things first."

"No time. You have to go now. It's not safe."

"Go ahead. I'll just be a moment."

Soon as the door slammed shut again, I rushed to join him. "What should I do?"

"I'll take you out the back way to the hangar and you can wait in the chopper just in case we need to leave. Then I'll help them put the fire out and hopefully avoid that outcome."

"Okay." I knew Dante had always had a plan for this eventuality. The helicopter was kept at the ready, in a specially built hangar behind the inn. But even he couldn't have anticipated a fire and someone storing flammable goods, maybe even illegally, I didn't know or care at the moment. I just wanted him safe.

When he bundled me into the aircraft, I laid a hand on his arm. "There's something I want to say. I love you. And you don't have to say it back."

"I should have said this before and I apologize for being commitment phobic. I love you, sweetheart, with all my heart and soul."

My whole being leapt for joy that my love was returned and I was hard pressed to let him out of my sight. But I had to stand by and watch him spring into action, though he turned back to acknowledge me one last time before vanishing from sight.

Chapter Nineteen

Dante

"Stay back, Mr. Luceres—it could blow at any second!" A burly man glanced my way as I stepped up to help. The town was without a regular fire department. A few volunteer members were on scene, pulled out of their beds during the frigid winter night.

"Mr. Aquilla, is it? I can help. I've had experience fighting fire before. I can handle one of the hoses since it looks like you're shorthanded."

"Tom. Everyone calls me that. Suit up, I have an extra one in my truck, and I'll put you to work. Though I'm not certain it will fit you—you're a big man." The guy sized me up with a glance. "The red Ford over there." Tom pointed out his vehicle.

I rushed over and pulled the thick black jacket from the front passenger seat with its broad yellow stripes with the large initials *UFD* branded across the shoulders. Back on scene, I was handed a heavy black hose with a silver nozzle attached and I went right to work, directing the heavy stream of frigid water at the bottom of the flames, joining others in the same action.

The men shouting orders at each other, the inhuman screech of fire consuming everything in its path, the black cinders raining down from the bomb fire — the whole world lit up with a frenzied energy. A section of the building collapsed, driving the firefighters back a few steps as the rush of live embers flew upward in a shower of sparks.

I was momentarily distracted from my job by the sounds of a high-pitched motor overhead. Looking up, I was stunned to see my own bloody helicopter moving away from the cloud of soot and ash. The rotors, spinning at high speed, dispersed the air above enough for me to see who was inside for a split-second of harrowing time.

Amara. No!

My body froze, knowing for certain the fire had been deliberately set to pull me away from her side. To give that asshole Akar his opportunity to wreak his vengeance.

"You okay, buddy?" Tom asked.

"What? No, I need to go. He's got her."

"Who's got her?"

I off-handed the man the apparatus and sprinted toward the inn just as the building they'd been dousing with water exploded again, sending debris raining down on everyone.

Cries of pain and fear struck my eardrums. I stopped in my task and looked back. The carnage was pitiful. I had to help, not even realizing I'd been hit with something before my legs collapsed under me and I fell to the ground. Darkness rushed in, claiming me.

Amara

I leaned back on the rich leather seat and instantly froze—a cold voice filled the space around me and pierced my unguarded mind that was so happy from hearing Dante's recent declaration of love for me that at first I could make no sense of it.

"Nice to see you again, Amara."

The smooth, unholy voice of Akar sucked up all the air in the helicopter. The contrast to the last few days made me unable to make a connection to any other thought for a few paralyzing seconds, my brain shutting down, overridden with apprehension and the beginnings of terror.

Finally, I found my wits as the vampire appeared in the cockpit in a blur of hazy movement. I struggled to undo my harness, but found myself unable to move, paralyzed by some trickery. A living nightmare descended as I attacked with the only thing I had left, my voice.

"What the fuck are you doing here?"

"I prefer my brides be chaste in deed and thought. No need for profanity. It is the last bastion of an uncivilized mind and displeases me."

"How the fuck did you find me?" I ignored his warning. He'd get a fishwife if that 'displeased' him so much. He did talk like he was from another century, not with it at all and too damned smug with his oily voice.

"Ah, but I am a man, or should I say, a vampire of my word." His sardonic comment gave me an overwhelmingly queasy feeling like he was trying too hard to be the gentleman he most definitely was not.

"And I promised to find you, so here I am. Ready and willing to be with you, even though you soiled yourself with a disgusting dog."

"How dare you call him that! You're not fit to wipe the shit off his boots, you stupid, disgusting motherfucker!" *There, choke on that word.* I hadn't used it before, but no holds would be barred now until I extracted myself from this mess.

"Tsk, tsk. I see you will require training. A muzzle may become necessary if you continue in this regard. This century has not done you any favors." While he spoke, he worked the controls, raising the hangar's electronic eye door and starting up the rotors on the aircraft.

My stomach turned as a question reared its ugly head. "Did you start the fire?"

"A useful diversion."

"How did you discover where I was hiding?" I asked the question again, unable to figure how with our being so careful, how a breach had occurred. Dante was such a thorough man, capable of the utmost security.

"I found an acquaintance of yours. Shay, I believe her name is?"

"Oh my God, you didn't hurt her? If you did, so help me I will tear you limb from limb and bury you so deep you'll never get out!"

I didn't care if what I said made any sense. I had lost it. No way was this vile creature going to get away with hurting my best friend.

"Your friend will stay safe and sound, recovering from a mind probe, if you cooperate," he threatened, his tone deadly. "Not that she knew much—that was bought and paid for by a disgruntled employee all too willing to sell me the intel on all the Luceres properties.

Never expected to have to come to this forsaken part of the world though," he growled, before working the controls to make the helicopter rise off the ground.

My spirits sank at the expanse of landscape revealed through the side window below us—a view of the inn and the fire raging next door. I searched frantically for Dante among the milling crowd. I spotted him at the same exact second he looked up and saw me. Our glances locked just before the copter swung sideways and headed for the darkened skies, Dante's look of anguish the last image burned into my retinas. I swore I heard his voice echoing in my mind.

"I'll find you, little one, no matter if I have to scorch the earth and lay it bare. I promise you that I will never let you go."

A living nightmare.

If I thought being bitten was the worst thing to happen to me, I had gotten it wrong. Unable to move a muscle and inhabiting a cabin with a vampire was far worse, so bad that a part of me wanted to throw myself out of the aircraft and see if I could fly. That was if I could only move. The thought gave me an idea. Maybe if I learn more about my abilities, I could turn the tables on the disgusting asshole to my right.

Crap. Some would say I was disgusting, being a vampire myself now. Dante had never made me feel that way, but right now, knowing I shared some of the same attributes with the vile menace working the controls, I felt sullied for the first time. I needed to shrug it off, stay focused and figure a way out of the situation.

"You have good timing," I said, gritting my teeth so hard at the lie I feared they'd snap off.

"How so?" He turned to look at me, his eyes glittering with interest. I forced myself to lift the corners of my mouth upward.

"I need to learn more about who I am. I imagine you can help me with that, right? A powerful vampire like you." *Appeal to his vanity, he looks like he's full of himself. Avoid swearing to antagonize the bastard, easy enough now that I had control of myself.* Shay would be proud of me, facing down a vampire, using whatever means at hand to turn the tables on him. I did it for her and for the love of Dante. This fell onto my shoulders to extract myself from. It wasn't my fault, of course, that I resembled this asshole's dead bride, but when fate sent a left hook, feign right.

"I will answer your questions. Keep you safe from that dog ever laying his hands on you again."

I couldn't bring myself to answer that in any way I could live with. Instead, I focused on outwitting my maker. Since the virus had infected my system some days before, I had been changing, growing stronger from my inner attributes that surfaced in surprising ways like my honed ability to write, so no way was this guy ever going to best me, not if it took the last breath in my body.

Thoughts of that made me realize I could break the chains of control holding me fast in my seat. I willed with all my might for my fingers to move, visualizing it. It hurt more than I could say, to lift my little fingers off my lap where my hands rested, but it did move! Just a little, proving I could regain control. That the monster who had created me would not have the last word.

"Where are we going?" I asked, needing to have points of reference.

"You look so like her now, with your platinum hair."

Okay. Not helpful. "I'm still adjusting. But you didn't answer my question." I worked at keeping my tone neutral.

"We'll be setting down soon, before the sun rises, and changing aircraft to an airplane that can fly us to our final destination. There will be a few stops along the way for refueling. I have minions that need not avoid sunlight to escort us."

He said that like I was supposed to be impressed. But his intel did tell me that we were headed a great deal of distance from North America. Where would an Egyptian vampire live? If I had to guess, somewhere near the pyramids or under them, perhaps in the Valley of the Kings near the city of Luxor. Just to have an awesome address to brag about.

"I've been told and have noticed that the virus you infected me with"—I just could not stop myself from the dig—"has changed many things about me. Speed being a plus. What else can I expect to have happen?"

"You should be grateful for the gift. Don't make me sorry. It won't end well for you. What I give, I can take away just as quick."

The threat was clear.

Bile rose in my throat. I glanced at his horrible pointed fingernails. *If you want a fight on your hands, lay one claw on me and you're toast.*

The radio on the aircraft sprung to life, drawing both our attentions.

"Be advised you are under surveillance. Turn the aircraft around or face serious repercussions." *Dante.* His voice filled the aircraft, fueling a flare of hope.

But all the vampire did was hit the radio transmitter with his fist and the device went silent.

"He can't do anything. And he certainly won't try to blow us out of the sky with you aboard. By the time he knows where you are, it will be too late," he gloated.

His words sent an ice-cold slice of fear through me. No. I had to believe.

"No more talking. Go to sleep," he commanded. I tried resisting it, but his will was strong and I decided to save my energy for the bigger fight that was sure to come.

Chapter Twenty

Dante

I slammed my fist into the console of the flight control deck. A counterproductive move as the instrument shattered into a number of impossible-to-reassemble pieces.

"I'll pay for it. Get another," I growled at the man in charge of the town's airport.

To his credit, the man didn't share the thoughts behind his scowl, but hurried off to do my bidding, arriving back with a portable device in no time.

"This will work. I'll give it a go for you. You need to rest. You took a hell of a hit, Mr. Luceres." The man whose name I had not bothered to learn set up the controls. My head ached like a drum corps was practicing their national anthem at the highest possible volume. I ignored it, though I had multiple wounds bleeding freely on my body that needed attention as well as a concussion. I could only focus on getting

Amara back. My body would heal in time, but not my heart if anything untoward were to happen to her.

"They're not answering my call. I suspect the device has been damaged in some way," the man said, his expression solemn.

"I need to get out of here. You have an aircraft I can buy? I'll pay anything."

"No need. I have a small Cessna you can borrow. I saw you helping at the fire. And I know your family's good for it. I'll have it prepared for you." The man scurried off again.

I needed all the help I could get. Was it time to call in the troops? Place myself at their mercy, knowing it might be futile? Was the slimmest chance they might be able to help worth it? They could hate me all they wanted for being with a vampire, but Amara had best be given respect.

She was trying to help their sorry asses after all, giving blood even when I cautioned her not too. Her zest to aid our cause for finding a cure for mortality endeared her to me in ways I could not fathom, though it was so much more than that drawing me to her. She was life itself, a woman to treasure over the ages. Her enthusiasm, great sense of humor, and yes, her beauty and grace, all captured my heart.

A scientist who now believed in Forever Mates. I didn't know when it happened exactly, just that it *had* happened. A life without Amara would be no life. I would find her, no matter how I had to beg, borrow or steal my way back to her. That I vowed with all I had or would ever possess. Nothing mattered without her.

I picked up the cell phone and made the call to my brother.

"Dante, where the hell have you been? There's a terrible riot going on within the family right now with your name attached. Lenore says you've hooked up with a vampire—*a vampire*. Tell me she's just shooting her mouth off?"

My brother Alejandro's voice filled the crackling airwaves with indignation. I sighed. "It's all true. And one hell of a story I'll share one day, but not now. I need your help. Can I count on you to have my back? I'm asking for her, Amara, my Forever Mate." I laid it all on the line. There was no time for easing in, not when everything was at stake.

"That's a lot to swallow. You do know you will be hauled up before the tribunal for this? You broke one of the sacred rules, mating with a vampire. What the hell's come over you? You've always been the most level-headed of all of us, voted the least likely to go AWOL. I mean you're a scientist, for heaven's sake. Me, they'd not be nearly as surprised considering my audacious history and general fuckupery. How on earth could this have happened to you?"

"Will you help me or not?"

"Of course, you're my brother. But you're making one hell of a mistake, for the record." Alejandro sighed.

"Thank you. I'm just about to leave Alaska. The bastard who bit her outside our casino has kidnapped her. He set a fire in the town as a diversion."

"Are you hurt?" My brother's voice instantly filled with concern.

"I'll survive. But it's Amara who needs our help—she was trying to help us."

"Help us? What do you mean?"

"Donating her blood for my research. I made a startling breakthrough, thanks to her and her

172

commitment. No time to get into it now, but she deserves our help more than you know."

"I'm not questioning *her*, just your sanity. But what do you want me to do? Gain the help of others? A few pack members I trust to keep it quiet?"

"Exactly." At that moment I realized how much I'd missed my brother. We'd been close growing up. It was just life had taken us in different directions. Alejandro was a playboy, straight and simple. He loved charming the ladies. He did have a heart of gold though and loyalty to a fault for any family member who asked, which was why I'd contacted him first.

Going forward, I wanted to spend more time with him, maybe discover more about why the guy was so notorious for playing the field. Especially knowing what I knew now and how much happiness could be achieved by finding the one we were meant to be with.

"We'll meet up with you wherever you say. Do you know where they're headed?" Alejandro asked.

"Only one logical location. Egypt. So I'm throwing all my cards on the table and heading there first. If I'm wrong, we can figure it out from there."

I filled Alejandro in on my basic plan and hung up, vowing to have my love back in my arms by any means necessary, even if it meant tearing the monster limb from limb.

Especially if it does.

"The bastard doesn't know what hell he's unleashed," I muttered, just as the owner of the airport came flying in the door.

Chapter Twenty-One

Amara

I awoke with a jerk. *Crap.* The nightmare was ongoing. I was now trapped in the back of an airplane behind a solid wall that stood between us and the pilot, with all the windows blacked out since I'd been transferred to the new mode of transportation in Gander, Newfoundland.

Been transferred by a vampire. I should have filled my pockets with garlic the night we'd gone to the casino, maybe prevented this whole damn thing. But then I wouldn't have met Dante who had brought so much joy and love to my life.

"We will be changing our mode of transportation shortly," Akar said.

I sat up straighter, observing Akar through narrowed eyes. *Untrustworthy. Vile. Evil to the core. Stinks of death.* There weren't enough words to sum up what I thought of him. My fists clenched at my sides. To think what he had done to me. It was no gift, if that was what he thought. It was not wanted, uncalled for and I would resist it any way I could if given a choice. I wanted to be like Dante, if my destiny was to be a supernatural creature.

Akar looked sweaty to me. I discovered why a few seconds later why when he hauled out the paraphernalia to snort cocaine. A mirror, credit card and bag of white powder appeared on the console. No wonder he was half mad.

"Want some?" he asked, his eyes glittering.

"You're kidding, right?" I asked in disbelief, unable to hide my sneer at his weakness.

He shrugged and went about snorting the shit up his nose.

I wrapped my arms around to hug my body that had begun to ache. "I don't need anything from the likes of you."

"You shall soon feel the power of the Bloodcall. A valuable lesson in humility awaits you." His maniacal smile set me off.

"Bloodcall? Is that what you call it when you attack innocent humans?" I could have bitten my tongue. *Focus on making the asshole an unsuspecting ally, not an out-and-out enemy, Amara. The drugs will make the beast even more unstable.*

"The Bloodcall consumes all of us. If left unchecked, it will cause mayhem that the Vampire United Federation will not tolerate. Think you're any better than the rest of us? Think again."

"I haven't drunk blood, if that's what you're asking, and I don't intend to." Or had I? What was in that amazing concoction that left me feeling top of the world? "And how is it you were able to attack me? If this — what did you call it — Vampire United Federation is so against the Bloodcall?"

"You are my long-lost love come back to me. All species know about love. It is the highest pinnacle of achievement a being can strife for. As important as the Bloodcall."

I did not want to be part of this world and I vowed never to accept its tenets or limitations. "Just because someone looks like someone else, it doesn't make them the person you're wanting them to be. That's a bit shallow anyway, thinking it's all about looks. You'd be better off searching for a new love. Maybe among your own kind, one who returns your interest? I think you'd have far more success that way. Or have you considered dating sites?" I spoke with a genuine regard for democracy — it sounded like the vampire world was more a dictatorship.

He looked at me like I had grown horns. "You are my kind now! And no more of this psychobabble. You will recognize the honor of being chosen or I will break you."

Yeah, right. Where did they grow them like this? Now I was worried the virus could affect me in ways still unknown. Over time, if I took it as a possibility that one lived for centuries, did a being become more delusional? Was it too much for the brain to handle? Or maybe it was the cocaine fucking with him?

"I have a few questions," I needed to think about something else. *Something practical.* "Does garlic keep vampires at bay? I know they can cross running water since we've passed lots of it on this journey, but what can kill one? You know for real, not what they say in movies or books."

"We have highly sensitized olfactory senses, so yes, garlic causes an allergic reaction. Some of the lore is correct in modern literature. Like beheading will end us or any creature. A stake through an un-beating heart, no, but it will leave a hole that takes a lot of blood nutrients to heal. We have to be very selective about live donors. Far easier to use a blood bank. Sunlight burns like living hell, but again, find a safe place and you will heal. Rejuvenation is something to observe," Akar replied.

"Do you use a substitute in place of drinking blood?" I asked.

"Many have been tried, few have worked. And none have prevented the Bloodcall for more than a few days. Most vampires make deals with blood banks or have one of their own servants working there to provide for their needs. Some humans volunteer as well." His sardonic grin sent icicles racing down my spine.

"I've never had real blood since I was turned. Dante makes a special concoction for me." What I wouldn't give for some right now. My mouth watered as I remembered the experience of the nectar sliding down my throat and sinking into my stomach. "I've never experienced this so-called Bloodcall," I said.

I got him. I saw the spark of sharpened interest in the creature the moment it happened.

"Is that right? Perhaps I have underestimated the cur in this one thing."

"Dante is a fine scientist." Miffed at the slur on my love, I directed my glare away from the loathsome creature.

"We have arrived."

The motors were indeed changing in tempo as the pilot pulled back on the throttle.

I felt the tires hit the runway, an easy landing, then come to a complete halt, before a voice came over the intercom.

"Mr. Akar, we have landed and your limousine awaits nearby. I will have the walkway placed directly and alert you when it is done."

Akar drilled his fingers on the armrests, looking impatient.

The captain's voice came again. "Everything is in place now, Mr. Akar. Please proceed forward at your preference."

"Very deferential pilot," I said, raising my eyebrows.

"He's a vampire wannabe. Easiest ones to control. They do our bidding until they realize they will never become one of us," Akar said with a curl of his lip.

"Rather unfair, don't you think?" I snapped, uncertain that I could ever manage in this world or why I would want to.

"Hope is a commodity, Amara. We need servants in this challenging world of sunrises and feeding complications. How else to survive?"

Was I supposed to feel sorry for his plight now, the poor, poor vampire? *Deadly night creature is more like it.* I would be haunted forever by that moment he launched himself at me, turning me without my permission into one of them. Only being with Dante kept the darkness at bay. His body and mind, so full of life and light...that was my hope for a better future. Helping him find cures for illnesses that struck so many without warning.

Because he not only helped his own kind, he worked at helping mankind as well. A worthy endeavor that had my utmost blessing and one I would definitely join him in as soon as I escaped this monstrosity. I had to believe it was possible, though a dark cloud threatened to swamp me. I had to be strong enough, smart enough and hopeful enough to keep it away.

"Time to go."

I unlatched my seatbelt and stood then stomped along behind him down to the covered skywalk, then the limo that whisked me away to parts unknown—the backseat had no windows, making a blackout curtain between us and the world.

"Where are we going?" I asked, keeping my voice level, trying to pretend I was calm.

"A safe haven awaits. You will thank me one day for this, rescuing you from those dogs. They would have turned you out, sent you on your way once your existence was discovered. Dante could not protect you forever from the centuries of bias against our kind. He'd have to bow to the common good or have his name struck forever from his pack. Shunned. And no wolf survives long without his familiars, even a scientist needs to feel part of something outside himself."

Shunned? The word was terrifying. Would my being with Dante be that costly to him? He had briefly mentioned that the species were enemies, but this, this was very bad. Worry hung heavy as a lodestone on me, attaching itself with suction-like tentacles to my brain. And just like that I was adrift in a sea of self-doubt with no shoreline in sight, my throat tightening with pain, making it hard to swallow.

I turned my face away to hide my emotions, tears slipping down my cheeks that I swept away with the back of my hand. If what the monster said was true, I had stepped over the line, no matter how unwillingly, and was now a pariah. How could I ask that of such a good man? To forever be turned out by his family? A family I knew he loved.

Being kidnapped and hauled to a distant land, that was nothing compared to what this news did to me, leaving me wretched and unable to cope for the moment. I wept silently, my lips pressed tightly together to avoid letting the vile creature next to me know what I was experiencing, the end of the dream of Dante and I and an amazing future. I now had to turn my back on an Eden filled with such promise, slip away from his life for his own good.

He had already gotten the best of me, I consoled myself. He had my blood that looked to give him and his family a cure for werewolf mortality, so at least there was that. He had my heart that would bear his image for all my existence.

But then why would I want to live forever? How could I without my love, with my heart bruised and my soul torn and bleeding. Was I being melodramatic, a small part of me wondered, digging down deeper painful as the sensation was?

No. My feelings are my own, not an exaggeration, they were what I was actually experiencing, and no one could tell me differently, not as long as I lived. *Once the heart is given, it's too late to pull back*. I knew that now. I was doomed to love him forever. Somehow, I would have to learn how to live without him.

The one thing I didn't know how to do.

Chapter Twenty-Two

Dante

We convened just outside Newark, an elite team of battle-scared wolves ready to do battle with the cold ones. My brother Alejandro had not let me down, bringing along the tools of the trade to assist their mission, along with five seasoned pack mates whose size and brawn spelled strength and power.

A new persona had come over me in the past few hours. Gone was the scientist and in his place rose a warrior ready to fight. A wolf who believed in the old myths and legends, who now had experienced their power. My Forever Mate was in danger and only I could see to her safety.

"You look like shit, brother. What happened to you?" Alejandro asked, pulling me into a tight bear hug.

"Good to see you too," I said, clapping my sibling heartily on the back. I nodded at the other men, a few members of my pack, Mateo, Sergio and Alfonso, all related by blood. A pack friend stood out, a Wulver of Scotland — one of our highland friends, Jamie.

I shook Jamie's hand, welcoming him. "Thank you for coming."

"I was visiting with Alejandro and when I discovered you needed assistance, well, here I am. Just point me in the right direction and let me at them!"

"I appreciate that. How's married life treating you?" Jamie had married a cousin of the House of Luceres under unusual circumstances last year that had looked like an abduction of the young girl until the situation had been explained.

"It's good."

I nodded. We'd all be a tight-knit group that could telepathically stay in touch during an assault, an ability essential for updating one other moment-by-moment, as needs could change on a dime.

"You brought along all the items I requested?" I asked Alejandro.

"That and more. Not taking any chances with these assholes. You owe me the whole story when this is over, bro."

"And you'll have it." I gestured with a nod of my head at the pack members while lowering my voice. "Do they know the situation?"

"Not exactly." Alejandro also spoke more softly. "The family is trying to keep it contained. The gig will be up when we find her and they realize Amara's one of them. We have until then to explain things."

"Okay, I understand. Let's roll. We need to attack as soon as possible, when they least suspect it."

"Egypt's a big country. Where first?"

"I know they have a permanent nest under the Great Pyramid of Giza, but I'm thinking that Amara's not capable of accessing the innermost chamber by shapeshifting to mist. Which leaves the Valley of the Kings near Luxor, Akar's old crib. His yet-to-be discovered tomb or another hidden one would be the most likely spot he'd hide her away until he teaches her what she'll need to know."

The thought of the evil one being in such close proximity to Amara was too much for me to think about for more than a few seconds of time. I needed to see beyond that, focus on getting her back.

"Sounds right. You want to fly the Lear or be my co-pilot?" Alejandro asked.

"I need the distraction. You deal with the flight plan and setting things up in Luxor," I said, striding with purpose across the tarmac before taking the stairs leading into the cabin of the plane two at a time. The pack members fell in behind me and hurried into the body of the plane, finding seats and keeping their usual rowdy comradery to a bare minimum.

Moments later, we were flying high over the Atlantic Ocean, my sights set on the country long considered one of the cradles of civilization. Disgust filled me. Such a beautiful country housing such vile creatures. If the citizens were aware, they'd riot in the streets. Unfortunately, there was no knowledge or access for humans to reach the innermost chamber, making the sanctuary the perfect location.

In mythology, Sekhmet, the legendary Egyptian feline warrior goddess associated with both plague and healing, was one of the oldest known vampire tales, as old as Lilith. The deity who began the blood lust was still being worshiped by Akar's minions. I shook my head. Education and science would lead the way to a better future, not ancient traditions that created chaos and suffering for others. But I did have something they wanted and was willing to trade. And if that was not enough, all guns blazing would suffice.

Scenarios of revenge for the terrible infliction foisted on Amara played in my mind, torturing me every second of the journey, keeping me alert right through the day and night and all the way to Egypt's shores.

As the sun rose over the River Nile, turning the waters golden for a brief moment, I maneuvered the aircraft down onto a runway near Luxor. All around me, the band of brothers — as I now thought of them for accompanying me on this dangerous mission — began waking up.

"Let's head into Luxor, check in and fuel up for a day searching the tombs," I said. I couldn't expect my comrades to be in top form without proper nourishment, as edgy as I was to just get on with things.

"Good idea, bro. I'm famished." Alejandro nodded. "The limousine's here," he added, looking out of the window at the tarmac.

"Thanks for arranging things," I said.

"We have rooms booked at the Grand Central Hotel. I left the reservation open, not knowing how long this will take. I also obtained special permission from the Minister of Foreign Affairs to conduct a search of the tombs that are normally closed to tourists. A guide has been arranged for us and will meet us at the hotel."

I could only pray that it would be a smooth turnaround trip and they'd be exiting the country in no time, though my stomach twisting into a tight knot belied the belief.

We disembarked the limo at the hotel and strode into the lobby. I found the hot dry air a cultural shock after the frigid air of the Arctic. Warmer, dryer air was a great deal more natural to the desert wolf I knew myself to be. But hell, I'd live in colder or hotter climes, if it meant being with Amara. Nothing would make sense without her in my life now.

"I'll meet you all in the dining room in five. I'm ordering the house special for all of us to save time," I said, my tone not allowing for dissension. Werewolves love to eat and choosing their food was a major pastime they relished. Groans followed my edict, which lessened when I returned their frowns with a don't-fuck-with-me glare.

"Just make sure to order lots and lots of food, Dante," Alejandro said, before hurrying to catch an elevator to take him and the other wolves up to the penthouse suite reserved for us.

I went in the opposite direction, to the restaurant, having no interest in anything else but getting on with things. After ordering enough to keep an entire platoon of men fueled for the day, I drummed my fingers on the tabletop, thinking through my plans one more time.

The advanced ground-penetrating radar system that my backpack contained had been enhanced to perform at even deeper depths and held the most promise for discovering Amara's location. I couldn't rely on our natural magnetic attraction to each other, strong as it was.

My backpack also contained a few meters of the tightest-weave fabric imaginable, material I'd designed that she'd wear to allow her safe transition to the limousine. Then the dark-tinted glass of the vehicle would also help on the way back to the hotel. I'd need to grease a few palms to keep Amara's identity secret, but that was easily done. I'd pay every cent I had at my disposal to have her back with me.

"Smells good in here," Alejandro said, joining me, rubbing his hands together. The others followed his lead and dived into the abundant feast, preparing for the hard day's work ahead.

"Napoleon Bonaparte said an army marches on its stomach. Never truer than of a pack of healthy wolves, right?" I said, pleased that I could provide for the men's comfort since they were there to help me.

It took courage to confront the cold ones, known for their long memories and vendettas against anyone who interfered with their plans. My mind dwelled on how much to share with my crew. Would they still be helping if they knew what Amara had become? And how was she doing without my special concoction? I had no answer for that. I ate without much appetite, but knowing I needed strength.

The sounds of cutlery hitting plates as food was scooped up and eaten in quick order and grunts of pleasure began to ebb after a few minutes and I stood up, throwing down a number of bills on the table to cover the tips for the attentive waiters.

"Okay, time to roll."

"I wonder where that guide has gotten to? He was supposed to meet us here," Alejandro said, looking around the dining room with a frown.

"I'm sorry, I was held up!" A middle-aged man came scurrying forward, his face creased in concern. "I'm at your disposal now as your guide for as long as you need me. Samir Bookman is my name." He bowed and we nodded, introducing ourselves to the animated guide.

The small man's dark skin was burnished by the sun, his loose clothing light in color and startling in contrast to the dark clothing of our crew. He wore mirrored sunglasses that were a bit off-putting. But he'd come highly recommended, according to my brother, so I'd give him the benefit of the doubt. No time to search for another guide to the tombs.

Packed into the limousine a few minutes later, I was impatient to get on site and the gear set up to hurry things along. Every minute without her was painful, like my heart was being ripped right out of my chest. Something the cold ones would attempt without a second's thought if they got a whiff of what I was about to do.

And what was that?

Take back the most precious female in the universe.

Chapter Twenty-Three

Amara

"Tonight, we take our rest here." Akar pointed out the spot, a rocky piece of ground that looked the same as any other shitty piece of land in the desert terrain. Where the hell were we? If this was the Valley of the Kings, I didn't recognize this area.

I frowned, confused. A wave of dizziness hit, making me work harder not to show any weakness to the monster. I made myself stand straight and tall. I would never let them know anything about me or who I was. *Let them guess, stew in the lack of information.*

He'd give up the game in boredom if I had my way, ditch me by the wayside somewhere to resume my life. The image bolstered me, imagining just being allowed to walk away from the deplorable situation. I'd find a cave and live out my life as a hermit. That was about the only choice left to me now. Maybe I was being melodramatic, but damn it, I had a right to it. My life had abruptly ended, thrown off course at someone's vile whim. I defy anyone to feel any different in my situation.

When I didn't bite and ask the obvious question, he pursed his lips at me, a calculating look coming over his feral face. He had the fine features of an aristocrat, a look I didn't like with its pinched nostrils and tight flesh.

"You think to freeze me out? I will hurt you very badly indeed if you don't respect me. I have ways of making you talk. Know all your thoughts if I have need, but out of regard for who you are, I have held off. Don't test me again, Amara. You have far more to lose than I have. Common courtesy is recommended in your case."

Roll my eyes or pretend obedience? Did it matter anymore? My thoughts darkened. What did I want most? Even though I could not ruin Dante's life with my presence? Yes. I still wanted to escape. And what best would allow that? Getting along with the creature until the opportunity presented itself was still the obvious option. But to do so would be demeaning. *Lousy frigging choices.*

Suddenly, while I was pondering the weighted decision, a figure appeared. A woman. A very beautiful woman with long dark hair who was dressed in a flowing white one-shouldered Greek-style gown, her expression devoid of any emotion. Too worried about wrinkles? Observing her did not buoy my mood any, but further derailed it.

"I see you have found her again, brother. Perhaps this time you can manage to keep her?" The sardonic voice had a resonance to it that raised the hackles on my neck.

"Sister, see to Amara's needs. Find her some fresh clothing and show her our ways."

She crooked a finger my way. "Come."

Was I just supposed to follow her like a toy soldier? I wanted to run and run and run. When I didn't move, I felt a sharp nudge at my back. When I whirled around to check what had happened, nothing or no one was near enough to touch me. It was as creepy as hell. They could fuck with my mind.

Not wanting to be invaded again, I stomped off after the soulless female who glided across the expanse on some kind of air current, wishing I had the courage to throw myself at her and take her to the ground, to upset all that grace and elegance she was currently displaying. Shay probably would have. She had huge lady balls.

"What size are you?" the creature asked.

"Clothes are the least of my concern. I really don't care if they fit or not. Any old thing will do."

"Akar cares. You represent us now. You look good, we all look good."

"Who's going to see me anyway, way out here?" I gestured with a wide-thrown arm at the landscape. "The bloody place is deserted."

"You will be meeting others soon enough. And trust me, appearances are everything to our kind. First impressions count. Tonight, we will deal with such matters. You are upset. Today you rest."

Her voice carried back to me as I followed along behind her, rolling my eyes at worry over such trivial affairs. *They have centuries to live and they worry about how they look instead of doing something useful with their time?* I was definitely on the wrong team.

"Where do I rest, exactly?"

"I'm taking you there now."

The landscape still looked barren to me, with few identifying features.

"This is the tomb prepared for your arrival." She stopped abruptly and I almost banged into her.

"Tomb? No, I don't want to do that." My body vibrated with disgust at the idea. "Is that the best you have to offer?"

"Well, if you had any training, you'd be housed in the finest surroundings. But you don't, and until you do, this will have to suffice." She pointed toward a cave-like entrance in the bedrock. I shook my head and backed up a few steps.

"Trust me, the owner doesn't care. They've been gone for millennia. Come. There's no time for delay, the sun is about to rise."

"Is this ground near Luxor?" I asked, trying to get my bearings.

"Why would that matter to you? You're just another pretty plaything for Akar."

"You know for sister and brother, you don't look much alike."

Selena stopped moving and turned around to face me. I found no shared facial characteristics in common with Akar.

"That's because we are not related. I am his first bride. One of the oldest of our kind in existence."

"Then why does he call you sister?" Perplexed, I stood my ground, refusing to follow her until I had some answers. *And to delay the inevitable.* I knew they could do with me as they wished and that thought terrified me if I allowed myself to dwell on it, so I didn't.

"Just our way. You will meet all your sisters soon enough. At the ceremony."

"What ceremony?"

"You must keep your distance from Akar until you are joined by him in a sacred union after you are trained. I pulled the short straw."

I ignored her taunt. I had not allowed my mind to think that far ahead, to having to be with him. I'd fight that tooth and nail. "How many are there like you?"

"Enough with the twenty questions. Come. I'll show you the way. Unless you want me to demonstrate our power again by shoving you all the way inside the chamber?"

Eww. "No thanks." I pulled on my best cloak of courage and ducked down at the entrance, following the dark creature inside the rockface, wishing it was a hotel or even a seedy motel rather than a dreaded tomb of the undead.

The air changed the farther we moved forward inside the enclosed space. From desert dry to moist and heavy with a slight scent of salt tasted before I swallowed. We took a hook to the left and continued onward. Just how far was it? The press of stone and earth above gave me a creepy feeling I couldn't will away.

"It's a tight squeeze ahead," Selena remarked.

The thick walls were covered with symbols — hieroglyphics. Not nearly as elaborate as some of the more well-known tombs, but still fascinating, but I didn't stop to study them. I didn't want her to have any excuse to touch my mind ever again. I shuddered at the memory of being shoved outside the cave.

"Where's the opening?" I studied the wall, seeing nothing but a plentitude of the same writings carved into the rock, though the channel had narrowed to the point the roof of the chamber was barely above our heads.

She laid her hand over one of the symbols in one spot then one in another and pressed. A grating sound came and a space began to open up near our feet. It stopped about a meter off the ground.

"You expect me to crawl in there?"

"Yes."

"Are you coming?"

"I will lead the way." This should prove fun as she would have to bend down and look ungraceful for the first time. Instead of bending though, she vanished, my eyes picking up a slight trail of fog or mist that disappeared almost instantly. Right, she knew how to shapeshift. I didn't. I bent down and wormed my way inside.

Standing up again, I dusted myself off, clapping my hands to my jeans and shirt. How I longed for a shower.

"I take it there's no running water in this joint?"

"You try to be funny, but trust me, none of us will be impressed."

Did I detect a slight impatience? "Well, I for one am not impressed by any of this. Why have you not built something better than this rat hole?" *Crap.* Where there rats here? I probably should have kept my mouth shut. Now I would be worrying about that until sunset. At least there were two raised areas for sleeping, covered with what looked like a mattress and a duvet. *Can rats climb?*

"If you had trained as one of us, we could stay at the finest accommodations in the Giza pyramid. But no, you chose to run away with a dog."

"He's not a dog, but the finest man alive. Just so you know, I will never stop trying to escape."

"You are a foolish one. You've been gifted by being created by a pharaoh and yet you moan like a child." She shook her head in disgust. "Go to sleep. I'm done with you tonight. Tomorrow we work on your ignorance."

"Ignorant! I'll have you know what is ignorant, turning a human to a vile creature against her will!"

She refused to be goaded, instead just lying down on one of the beds, turning her back on me.

"You disgust me, you piece of —"

Suddenly I could not speak anymore, my voice box incapable of saying anything. *Fuck.* This was annoying. *They don't like what I have to say and they just stop me from saying it?* What had happened to the idea of democracy in this crew? The sooner I could get away from these monsters the better, even though I had nowhere to go.

I too was a monster, or could become one without Dante's continued help. Tears slipped down my cheeks while I silently mourned. Was this it? My fate was to become one of them?

I began to pray that I would find the strength to escape. I just needed one tiny opportunity and I would slip through that crack if it killed me.

Because death was preferable to this horror.

Chapter Twenty-Four

Dante

We had been searching with the ground-penetrating radar for hours without success. Soon it would be dark and the vampires would rise, making the job that much more difficult.

"Do you think maybe we were wrong? That they headed to Giza instead?" Alejandro asked, his face pensive.

"No, I think she's here. Let's try farther out that way, toward the oldest tombs. They're less elaborate in structure, but still capable of containing secret compartments."

I squatted down and rolled out the huge map onto the ground, quickly adding Xs to every stop we'd ruled out.

"The guys are beginning to ask questions."

"Yeah, like what?" Distracted, I didn't pick up the inflection on my brother's voice.

I glanced over at him. Alejandro looked uncomfortable, hesitant to say.

"It's about why a vampire would bring Amara to Egypt, right? They think it's too late, that she's been turned already." It was easy enough for me to guess.

"Yes, so they don't see the point of it all. I need to know, why this particular vampire? You say you think she's your Forever Mate —"

"I don't think. I know." I softened his curt words with a nod of understanding. "Trust me, she's very important in many ways. Like I told you, her blood is offering us a better future."

"In what way?" Alejandro pressed.

"Living longer. Her blood has aided my research, making it possible for me to create a vaccine that will extend our lives. I'm not certain how much just yet, trial studies are needed, but it looks promising."

"And then we all turn into vampires?"

"Who's turning into a damn vampire? That woman, Amara, is she one of them now? We might as well give this up then, if we're no longer needed." Jamie had come closer during our talk, eavesdropping on the conversation. I clenched my fists.

"This is none of your business, Jamie. Leave it alone."

"It is if you think we're going to leave here with a vampire in tow," Jamie blustered, his face turning even redder than the sun had already made it.

"She's not one of them. She's my Forever Mate. So, if you can't get your mind around that —" I stood, confronting Jamie.

"Dante," Alejandro cautioned. He turned to speak to our cousin. "Jamie, Amara is very important to Dante and to our pack. She's been assisting my brother with research, helping discover a treatment for mortality. Seems we all may be able to live longer soon as Dante makes the vaccine available."

"Is this true, Dante? Have you had a breakthrough?" Jamie's facial expression changed to one of wonderment.

I nodded. "I'm very close to being able to create enough vaccine to inoculate our first test subjects."

"Great! You need test subjects, I'm your wolf," Jamie said.

Could it be this easy? Would the rest of the pack support our relationship since Amara had so much to offer them? I wanted them to want her for who she was and what she stood for, to accept my decision as a full pack member in choosing her, not just because she could be of physical use to them. But at least it was a start.

"What's all this about test subjects? You onto something, Dante?" Mateo came up, his normally brooding look one of keen interest.

"Yes, Amara is the source of the vaccine that will be able to extend our lives."

"But she's a vampire, right, one of those disgusting cold ones?" Mateo asked, his expression changing to one of horror.

"Come closer and say that!" My ire fired to red-hot in an instant. I was ready to fight, take them all on if necessary.

"You defending vampires now?" Mateo asked, his eyes narrowing down to mere slits. "Fuck, I'm out of here and so should all of you. Never thought I'd see the day that a Luceres would lower themselves to such an extent that we'd go in aid of a damned vampire."

Before I could slug him, he strode away, his back stiff with outrage.

I watched him have a heated discussion with Alfonso and Sergio at a distance before the trio left together without a backward glance.

"We don't need them," Alejandro said with conviction.

Jamie nodded. "No, and I wouldn't bother to share the vaccine with them when the time comes either. But our highland clan would appreciate the medicine."

"You'll have it. You have my word. Now let's get on with this," I said, needing desperately to focus on what was right here, right now, because the future was looking further away by the minute. Without the others' help, the chances of success on our mission had lowered considerably, a fact I was going to ignore. And if anything were to happen to my brother, I would never forgive myself.

"I want you both to leave once we find her. I can't worry about your asses being on the line when or if a battle ensues." Of course all hell would break loose. Akar would never give up his prize without a fight. And he didn't even know just how precious a find she was.

"No fucking way, bro. You can't get rid of me that easy. I'm staying and that's all there is to it," Alejandro said.

"I will stay as well. A Highland Wulver loves a good fight," Jamie added.

I would just have to find a way to keep Alejandro safe and out of the loop. Hard as it would be, when I discovered Amara's whereabouts—I wouldn't allow myself to think any different—then I would wait until I was alone to confront the enemy.

"Where's that guide gotten off to now? I'll be back," Alejandro said, grumbling about the man as he strode off to find him.

Samir Bookman had been of little use, seeming to vanish for long periods of time. Maybe he was needing a bracer? The man had the look of a drinker about him, his eyes bloodshot when he'd briefly removed his sunglasses to read a map.

It dawned on me that it would be an undiscovered tomb as yet that would most likely have been chosen by Akar. A small, obscure resting place would best fit his needs of staying hidden in plain view. I needed to go beyond the obvious, work the edges of the valley well beyond the spectacular tombs already documented by his crew.

Damn. I should have thought of this before. I strode off the beaten pathway and over unchecked land farther to the southwest, hoping to find even a hint of where Amara was hidden. It was hot, tiring work, but I ignored my body's calls for water, too distracted and worried about her to care.

"Drink this," Alejandro said sternly, appearing at my side. He thrust a water bottle at me. "You have to take better care of yourself, bro, if you're going to be of any use to Amara."

I downed the entire two-liter bottle in one go. "Thanks."

"I hate to say this, but maybe she isn't here?" Alejandro said, his tone neutral.

"She's here! She has to be."

"It's going to be dark soon. We can try again tomorrow. Samir was able to extend our visa by another day."

"That's good, but I'm not leaving her."

"Then put this on if you're going to stay after dark." Alejandro handed me a thick garland of garlic bulbs. He already had a pungent one circling his own neck.

"Fine." I knew the value of garlic in repelling the cold ones. Due to the chemical composition of the blood disorder that caused vampirism, garlic was the only known way to sicken a vampire who came too close. Most novels got that part right. None of the religious artifacts helped, unless they were made of silver, the other known vampire repellent. Unfortunately, the garlic could also make Amara ill.

I'd throw it away and bathe soon as possible after locating her. I was more worried about getting her some of the special drink I'd created. Each second without the essential nourishment meant she was a ticking bomb.

"Why are you wearing those?" Samir suddenly appeared, pointing with disapproval at the garlic bulbs circling their necks.

"Just happen to love the invigorating fragrance," I said with a tight smile.

Samir's eyes narrowed. "It will be dark soon. Perhaps it is time to retire to the hotel?"

"You go on ahead. We'll join you shortly."

"It is prohibited to remain in the area after dark," Samir said, his disapproval obvious.

"We have a few more minutes. Go. We'll catch up. I want to talk to my brother alone," I said, my tone dismissive. Why was the man deciding to do his job now after being absent most of the day?

After a moment of indecision that was written all over the man's face, he turned and strode off.

"Okay." I took a deep breath. "Let's get at it. Time is running out. If they rise at dusk, they may leave the area."

The sun was just a finger's width above the horizon and sinking far too fast. I strode over the parched land as fast as I could, holding the radar equipment in my right hand, moving it back and forth like I was holding a broom. Each sweep would cover a few meters either way, and the readout immediately digitized and reported onto the laptop that my brother held, watching for any bodies under the soil.

The clock ticked in my head, each second that passed a lost opportunity. *God, please let me find her. I'll even start going to church if you just give me a sign,* I prayed, giving up my agnostic beliefs in barter. Whatever it took, I had to find her. I could not imagine a life now without Amara.

"Stop! I see something," Alejandro cried as the sun slipped below the horizon, the laptop's screen gleaming in the encroaching darkness.

"Where?" I demanded, frantically searching the image for what my brother had found.

"There. Just a few feet back. Under that rise in the landscape." Alejandro jabbed with a finger at the area on screen. "One body, fully fleshed. Not bones like the others."

We'd already located a few unknown tombs with the advanced software unavailable to any others on earth, leaving them for archeologists to find at a future date. The House of Luceres didn't need the glory or the hassle of explaining how we'd discovered the burial grounds of more pharaohs, and particularly the unknown pharaoh, Akar I, born well before Ramses. A holy terror, now and when he ruled ancient Egypt, so many millennia ago. No wonder his name had been struck from the annals of history.

"Yes! It looks right!" My heart rate jacked up with the realization that I was possibly within moments of rescuing my love. "Let's go!"

I stalked toward the entrance of the hiding place, too focused on finding Amara to notice a slight shift in the air. Then it was too late. A half-dozen cold ones blocked my way, their menacing teeth and claws gleaming starkly in the darkness.

"Bring it on, you bastards. I'll rip you all to shreds," I taunted, assuming a fighting stance. A part of me relished this, but another part wanted this to be finished, yearning desperately to be with Amara.

"Give it up, cur, you're outnumbered," one of them growled, his tone menacing.

I noted though he was being cautious, not just jumping into the fray. Could they smell my newly heightened powers? I had made the most of my chemistry through hard work and labor. I deserved every ounce of gain over these bastards. I had to end this. Now.

"The odds are in my favor. Prepare to die," I said, leaping forward through the metaverse as I said it, striking down two of them in one swoop, decapitating both with my sharpened claws, arms outstretched. No longer the scientist, I was the wolf, the warrior, an advanced fighting machine created with brilliant tactics, prepared for any battlefield. I had never been so large, so strong, so fully capable of handing out death. I relished the power.

No one fucks with this Luceres. I understood my kind like never before. We'd had to fight for centuries to find our way. The glory was I had taken that and made us even more. Made us the best, the most lethal predators on earth.

The remaining four looked at their fallen comrades then turned their attention on me, all four circling me, far more cautious than before.

"Akar too cowardly to fight along with you? You just do his bidding?" I telegraphed, looking for my chance to take out two more.

"You will pay for that," one warned.

"Prepare to die!" I said, ready to attack again.

Before I could, Alejandro and Jamie rushed the group, their wolf forms strong and menacing as they leapt to do battle with them. *No.* I wanted to do this myself. *Keep my brother and pack member safe.*

I leapt in, striking two more of the bastards, knocking both to the ground. I slashed with my claws, damaging the first beyond saving, the second one crawling away like a pathetic baby.

My brother had another in a death grip, his teeth sunk into the throat of his opponent, his massive head shaking back and forth as the vampire's life force drained into the sand.

One to go. I nodded at Jamie to leave the dog to me, then grinned at my final opponent. He looked uncertain, glancing this way and that. I rushed him and bore him to the ground.

"Give up and you will live. Go back and tell your master he's made a huge mistake in coming after my woman. Try again and I will unleash hell on all of you!"

The vampire nodded, his eyes widened by fright. Blood smeared his face from my holding him around the neck. The rank odor of fear filled the air.

"I will. Have mercy. Please, I beg of you!"

Chapter Twenty-Five

Amara

I awoke with my heart thudding and my memory flooding with recent events. The rock ceiling above my head proved I was still in the damn tomb, still stuck with one of Akar's women. The creepy Selena.

When I turned to look at her, expecting her to be lying on the bed opposite in all her glory, I discovered she was gone. Where had she gotten off to? I staggered to my feet, my stomach squeezing painfully, reminding me I hadn't eaten anything in the last twenty-four hours.

It was torture to be alone in the chamber, sensing the dead souls that had come and gone for thousands of years in the valley. I worked my way all along the rough wall, checking with my fingers for a switch or button to push but finding nothing. Selena had made it look so easy to come and go. What I wouldn't give for some of her specific knowledge. What time was it anyway? It seemed an eternity had passed waiting in this dead zone. Was this it? Was I going to be left to die in this place?

I sank down on the floor in despair, my back to the wall. I had been so happy the last couple of days, even working alongside Dante in the lab. Why had it come to this? What meaning was there to having this happen to me? Okay, I was supposedly cured of my former illness, that was huge and definitely on the pro side of the page. But the con side held more items. Gifted with an unimaginable love affair then to just have it yanked out from under me, that was the worst con of all.

I wasn't a poor-little-me type, but sitting there in the semi-darkness, life sucked big-time.

What Akar had said about Dante being shunned — was it true? If so, I could not bear the thought of coming between him and his family who he loved. No, never could I let that happen. I had to be the bigger person, let him go, as much as it would cause me the kind of pain I could barely imagine at the moment. A pain I must endure because I could not be the cause of the downfall of a great man.

A horrible sensation began growing within me, an itch under my skin, an itch I couldn't get rid of by scratching, try as I might. I stumbled to my feet and began pacing, whirling about every few steps to go back the other way. I swear the damned walls were closing in on me.

"I can't stay here!" I screamed the words aloud at the top of my lungs. "For heaven's sake, let me out of here!"

Faint sounds, a scratching, stopped me. What was that? I cocked my head to the side, listening. Had someone come for me? I worked to calm myself.

A small black flexible cord appeared between a small crack in the floor and the wall where the space I had crawled through earlier had been, drawing my attention. Who was outside? I grabbed hold of the cord and checked it out, pulling it farther inside the tomb. A digital camera perhaps? Peering at it, I hoped I was correct as to its usage. Because if it was, someone on my side had to be here to help, right?

Dante

"Look! She's staring right into the camera!" I half-shouted, my glee at having found Amara brimming over. Her digital photograph filled the laptop screen, bringing a warm rush to my chest. A more beautiful picture I could not imagine. But the torment of being so close yet unable to touch her —

"She's a beauty. I'll give you that, bro. Unusual hair color, very striking."

"Damn effects of the virus. Now how do we get her out of there?"

"There must be a hidden switch or something."

I began to press with my hands and slam my fists against areas of the wall, impatient to get inside and rescue my love. "Damn, how does this fucking thing work?" I swiped at the sweat beads dripping from my forehead, the sting in my eyes momentarily blinding me.

An alarm began to sound, shrilling loudly. Too high-pitched for humans, but a sound that would drive supernaturals to their knees.

Ka-boom!

An explosion ripped through the chamber right at us, tossing me through the air to land on my back a good distance away. I shook my head, blood dripping in my eyes, the stench of hellfire in my nose, my eyes blinded by dust. Could I move my limbs? Every cell in my body screamed with pain. My God! Where was Alejandro? Jamie was guarding the outside entrance, but Alejandro was with me.

Ignoring the pain stabbing up from my foot, I crawled forward, trying to reach my brother. A weak groan caught my ears. I pushed myself to move quicker, my limbs on fire. He had to be okay.

"Dante…"

The voice focused me. My brother had fallen closer to the edge of the rockface, his body half invisible. Was he dying? Had he lost some limbs? I would never forgive myself if that were true. I dragged myself forward on my elbows to get to his side, then discovered he was half-off a ledge, blown there by the bomb going off. There was now a huge chasm between us and the door to Amara.

"Are you okay? Can you move at all?" I asked, gingerly taking hold of his head.

"I think so. Just knocked the wind out of me."

I grabbed his shoulders and dragged him away from the edge. When we were safely back, I checked Alejandro over more carefully. Though he was covered in dust and spitting mad, his limbs were undamaged. Like me, he was covered in myriad flesh wounds that bled freely, staining the dust black.

We sat together, staring at the deep chasm. I tossed a large rock over the side, hearing a faint answering sound a few seconds later. It was fucking deep.

"What do you think?" Alejandro asked.

"I need a ladder. There looks to be just enough rock on the other side, if I lay it down, to cross over. Bit dicey, but it should hold me. And I think the door came up enough that I can squeeze my way in." Not an enticing maneuver. Would it close down on my chest, killing me? I had to risk it.

"Crap, Dante, that's a pretty iffy proposition. You must love her beyond all reason. There could be more booby traps waiting."

"Doesn't matter. I'd walk through hellfire for her." I didn't bother calculating the odds in my head. I figured I was better off not knowing.

"You may have to."

Leaving my brother on guard, I stumbled back down the tunnel to get outside the tomb, each step an agony with my broken foot. It would heal soon enough, but not in time to be of any help this night. I had to get her out of there before daylight. Otherwise, who knew what could happen?

Jamie waited at the entrance, his expression turning to shock when he saw the state I was in.

"Wait here and guard my brother," I instructed. "I'll be right back."

I located a ladder inside the back room of the gift shop, bore it up on my shoulder and shambled back to the tomb as quick as possible, one foot dragging. At least I didn't meet any of Akar's minions on the journey. My initial attack had no doubt scared them off.

Moments later, I lay the ladder across the twelve-foot divide, careful to position it at the shallow advantage point in front of the partially upraised doorway. A scant ten inches was exposed at the bottom of the heavy stone door, maybe enough to get through? More importantly, was it booby trapped? What next? A flood or a nail-studded coffin?

"I need a crowbar or something to brace it or try to lift it upward if I don't fit. Could you try to locate one?"

"I don't want to leave you. What if you fall, need my help, bro?" My brother shook his head, his expression grim to the extreme. "A crowbar would take time to locate."

"Then I will just have to risk it." I set my resolve and began the awkward trek across the chasm. *Don't look down*. Not a fan of heights, I took it one step at a time.

*Arm outreached, grasp rung of ladder, slide my body forward...*trying not to drag my foot or dislodge the slim margin that device was precariously poised on. I did feel like Indiana Jones, minus the snakes. Then of course I imagined them raining down on my head from above or some other such shite. *Focus.*

Sweat dripping in my eyes, my teeth aching though my ankle throbbed the most, I crept across, one rung at a time. Finally, I was close enough to peer under the doorway. I couldn't see anything moving under the thick ledge of rock for all the debris that had tumbled down. My God, was she hurt from the blast? Lying under a ton of rocks on the other side? My heart clenched so tight I was certain I was having an attack.

"Amara," I called out. "Are you okay? I've come for you, sweetheart. Please, say something if you can hear me."

A soft moan gave me hope.

"Can you get through the debris?"

No answer. I looked back at my brother. "I'm safely across now and I need something to dig with. Go. Look for a crowbar."

"I'm on it."

But I wasn't waiting for tools. I just didn't want Alejandro to see me fall if it came to that. I began digging, pulling chunks of rock away from the opening and letting them drop down the chasm. It was a grim task, made more difficult by my needing to stay perched on the ladder. The space in front of the opening simply wasn't big enough for me to move off my means of access.

"Can you see me now?" I asked, bending and peering through the cleared opening. It wasn't large enough yet for me to slip through.

"Yes," she said, her tone so weak I wanted to bring down the entire wall of rock on Akar's fucking head. Was she experiencing hunger or pain? Either was intolerable. Not for one second should my Forever Mate not have the very best care. My wolf struggled to be free to hunt the vampire down, but I suppressed the urge.

"Can you move? Are you hurt?"

"No."

"Dante!" my brother called out. I turned around and grabbed the crowbar in mid-air. The adrenaline charge of thirty men filled me as I tore into the rock face keeping me away from Amara, dislodging huge chunks of heavy granite that dropped off into the darkness below. The strike of steel on stone set off a series of thundering clashes that threatened to alert all of Luxor to the activity. I didn't care and pressed onward. I would save Amara or die trying.

Finally, the entrance was widened enough for me to make my way inside underneath the heavy stone wall. I looked around frantically. Amara was lying down on a pallet, white as a ghost. The tomb was not nearly as damaged inside as the tunnel leading to it, the blast meant to project outside, I realized in a moment of clarity and thankfulness.

I dashed to her side and swept her into my arms, holding on for dear life. "Are you okay, sweetheart?" I asked.

"I am now."

I wasn't so certain, feeling her body trembling. "I have something for you." I pulled the heavy plastic vial from the belt I'd strapped around my waist and opened it for her, thankful the blast hadn't punctured it. "Drink."

She did as I asked, gulping the sustenance in short order. She wiped her mouth with the back of her hand. "Thanks."

I crushed her to my chest again. "I'm never letting you out of my sight again."

She laughed nervously, her eyes not meeting his. "About that. We need to talk."

I didn't like the sound of that. "Let's get you out of here first."

"Ah, Dante, we need to be going," Alejandro said, his tone full of warning.

I assisted Amara through the small opening first, warning her to stay pressed against the wall, then squeezed through and joined her on the narrow ledge.

"I'll help you across the ladder. Don't be afraid," I said.

"I just won't look down," she said, the brave expression on her face making me so proud of her.

Rung by rung, she slowly made her way across the deep divide. I didn't dare breathe until she was safely on the other side, my brother helping her at the end. My turn next. I made my way to her, my actions sure.

"Okay, let's roll," I said, placing my arm around Amara.

"I'll take the other ride, bro, give you and Amara time alone," Alejandro said.

"Thanks for all you did tonight. I owe you big-time, you and Jamie."

"Damn right you do!" Alejandro said before striding away to join up with Jamie in the second car.

I helped Amara into the back of the first waiting vehicle, trying not to let her see me limp with my still healing foot. Driving through the star-filled night, Amara safe in my arms, my life made sense again.

Chapter Twenty-Six

Dante

"I don't want you to feel any pressure. But when you're ready to talk about all this, I'm here for you," I said.

"Now's not the time. Tomorrow would be better," Amara said, like a prisoner going into the dock.

I didn't like the sound of heavy strain in her tone. What the hell had Akar done to her?

"Are you sure you're okay? Did he hurt you in any way?"

She shook her head. "No, he didn't do anything to me. Well, other than kidnap me. But that's over now."

"Then what's wrong? Please, be honest with me. You're worrying me. You don't sound like yourself, sweetheart." As happy as she was to be rescued, I sensed something far deeper was in the way of our having a truly happy reunion.

She sighed, as if the weight of the world was held up by her slender shoulders.

"I love you, Dante, but it's not enough. Look at how hurt you are. You're covered in cuts and bruises and you're limping. I can't bear it, that he hurt you."

"What on earth do you mean? I'll heal, don't give it a second thought. Of course our love is enough. It's everything. Where is this coming from? Did Akar say something to you? Tell me. You're scaring me."

To admit how I was feeling was right out of character for me, at least the old me would never have admitted such a thing as acute fear.

"Is it true that vampires and werewolves are strictly forbidden to be together?" She looked me straight in the eyes as she asked the question.

"Don't worry about that now. We'll figure it out together. This comes from Akar, right? Don't let that bastard influence you. We will overcome all of this, no matter what it takes."

I had to soothe her. Akar was such an asshole, making her worry so much about something I was now determined to fix. And if it couldn't be fixed, then so be it. Amara and I were destined to be together, and fuck the rest of the world.

"What did he say to you?" I demanded. I had to eradicate all such thoughts, right now, before this cancer sank in any further.

She shook her head, her expression weary as she looked away, as if reciting something from memory. "I have too much baggage and come at too high a cost. I can't ask that of you. To never see your family again because of an ancient feud between our species. To be hounded by vampires that don't take no for an answer. In time, you would begin to resent me. I don't want that. I love you too much not to let you go. Surely you can see that?"

"All I can see is that without you, I have no idea how to move forward. You're everything to me now. You make me a better man, just being with you. So no, I don't see it and I don't accept it."

"It will be hard, I know."

Her tone of finality froze the marrow in my bones. I had to fight this, sway her, or everything would be lost. I dug down deep and began to speak from the heart, needing to persuade her with my words and conviction.

"Where's your courage? You don't sound like the Amara I've grown to love. The spunky one with the heart of gold. Don't do this to us." I had a moment of inspiration. "Did you know that my cousin married a full-blooded witch? It's time for a change, Amara. All species deserve to be accepted for who they are, what they represent. There are bad humans, bad wolves and bad vampires and fae and a host of others. It doesn't mean a whole group should be exiled for the actions of a few. I will fix this, you'll see. I think maybe if you talked to Isadora, our resident witch, you'll feel better. They know what it's like to be an outsider. But they have the courage of their convictions. If you give up this easily, then I have to ask if you ever really loved me at all?"

"Of course I love you! Don't say that!" She turned a tear-stained face toward me. "I don't know what I should do. I want you to be happy."

"Just don't give up on us. That's all I ask. Please, give it a little time to sort itself. I know we can do this. I can handle my family. And if they can't accept you for the incredible spirit you are, that's their loss. I won't—I can't accept that I would be asked to live my life without you."

"But how are we going to keep him from coming after us? You know he won't give it up. He's far too narcissistic and self-involved to ever let this go. He'll come after us when we least expect it. Start another fire or something like that. The second we take our hand off the throttle, he'll strike. That's no life, Dante, I can't ask that of you, having that blood sucker always at our heels. You deserve so much more than that."

"So do you. I'll plead our case to the powers that be. Everyone who's ever been in love has to understand. You fight for yours. It's time to change antiquated laws."

Amara sat up straighter, sparks glinting in her beautiful eyes. "I'm coming with you. Together we can make our case. At least then, if it doesn't work, I'll have no regrets."

"It will work. I'll set it up. Now shut up and kiss me!" I said, softening my alpha command with a devilish grin.

"My pleasure," Amara murmured before I pressed my lips to hers, breathing in her essence and feeling all those lovely curves against me, or at least as much as sitting beside each other would allow. She surprised me then, climbing up on top of me and straddling my lap, her thighs wide apart, our groins pressed together, a pleased grin lighting her expression. Heaven could not top this.

I quickly pressed the button that would raise the window partition and seal us off from the driver's view. We needed to be together now, reconfirm our love.

I ground myself against her core, wanting her like the earth needs the rain. I pressed harder, seeking the warmth within. My blood heated red-hot, coursing under my skin, tightening my cock until it felt about to burst free from my pants, hard as steel. A moan. A gasp. The outside world dropped away, making only this moment, this second, all that mattered.

She softened into me. I was lost in her, grasping a full breast and finding the nipple hard, budded. The warmth of the pliant flesh sent me reeling. God, I wanted her. Wanted to have her stretched naked beneath me, wet for me. Wanted into the very core of her. Make her forget all that had happened. What I would make sure never happened again, if it cost every cent I had and the calling in of every favor on the books.

"Amara," I murmured against her lips, "I have to have you. Now." Our breaths mingled, heating the air around us, obscuring the outside world as moisture formed, clouding over the windows.

My hands pulled at her clothing until she began to help, shucking off her shoes, jeans and panties in one frantic movement. I unbuckled my belt and pulled down the zipper and before I could get my jeans and boxers completely off, she was on top of me, centering herself over me, grasping my cock with one hand, thrusting me into her pussy. I slid inside, pushing past the slick, tight entrance to thrust up into her, pulling her down as far as I could, burying myself balls-deep inside her tight warmth.

"Oh, my God," I moaned, my cock straining for sweet release, my head swimming with the quickness of being inside her. I'd missed her so much in the past number of hours after having been together every moment. I lunged into her with my hunger, burying my face in her fragrant hair, working my hands over her naked breasts, pushing her bra cups down to make them jut out farther until she moaned against my mouth, wetness flooding her channel.

My body wasn't my own, my need beyond powerful. I forgot everything else, where we were, what was going on. I was rough, rougher than I had ever been with her. My hot cum rushed up from inside my balls, tingling and seeking release. Raw. Like I had never known. Harder than I had ever been. The acute desire for more overcame me, the primal need driven by an overpowering urgency to keep her safe. She was my addiction, my everything.

Claim her.

Mark her.

Make her ours.

My mouth sought her shoulder and my tongue licked the spot, sensing the exact location. *Now. We must do it now.*

In a flash of light, a strike of lightning, a chorus of distant howls.

"Claim me," she urged, like she knew my torment. "Make me yours forever."

No restriction remained. I needed no further urging. I bit down, tasting her sweet and wild essence flowing across my tongue, lifegiving.

She gasped. I licked the spot to seal the small wound. My scent would stay inside her forever.

"I'm coming," I growled, tugging on her nipples, reaching down and rubbing on her swollen clit, wanting her to reach orgasm with me.

I sucked one tightly budded nipple into my mouth, drawing hard and eliciting more sweet moans. I took a deep breath, my lungs about to burst as I forgot to breathe. The fragrance of sex filled the limousine, our scents mingling.

"I'm almost there," she shouted, slamming herself down on to me over and over, her breasts bouncing with each impact, her pussy squeezing me tight. A final thrust and we collapsed against each other, into each other, our breaths harsh in the confining space.

"Welcome home, sweetheart," I murmured, my lips against her cheek as she rested her naked chest against mine

"Good to be home," she said, her wicked, happy grin all the thanks I needed.

We rearranged their clothing and she slipped back into my arms, lying with her head against my chest.

"I think we need to consider sharing my blood with you. Then the mind connection between us will grow even stronger like it does for all pack members," I said, thinking ahead, adding, "And then he can never enter your mind again."

"Can I be vampire and werewolf at the same time? Is that a possibility?"

"We can do it slowly, test your reaction to it. I'd rather you all vampire, than take a chance. But there might be a way. I've been working on the problem. But enough of that for now. Tonight, we celebrate us."

Chapter Twenty-Seven

Amara

The day of the tribunal in Vegas came on the heels of a sandstorm, raging outside our suite in the Glitter Palace. I watched it play itself out over the Strip as I drank my morning coffee. It had driven everyone inside, leaving small piles of sand pressed up against buildings. Was this a bad omen?

Nervous, I finished my drink, then hurried to the bathroom, leaving Dante on the phone. I showered, then fidgeted in front of the bathroom mirror, trying to get my hair to behave. My abundant locks were not cooperating, sliding out of the pins meant to contain it.

"Damn it!" I slammed down the brush and glared at myself in the mirror.

Dante's face suddenly appeared beside mine, a frown marring the perfection of his tan forehead. "No need to fuss. Just leave it down. You're beautiful no matter what you do anyway."

I managed a weak smile. "I want to look professional. You know what they think of my kind as it is?"

"You are my kind."

"Right! That's why you had to vouch for me, that I wouldn't go in all bloodthirsty and ready to attack the innocent. And why can't I change into a wolf? I've tried so many times and it doesn't work!"

That still stung. Dante had shared a little of his purified blood in the lab with me, but maybe not enough for me to be able to shift? Good thing it wasn't medieval times—I could see myself being hauled in an iron-barred cage or something equally humiliating.

"Don't worry about that. Once they meet you, listen to what you have to say, all that will be gone. They will love you just like I do. And if they don't, I will take you far away. I will never leave you again, sweetheart. It would be the death of me."

I turned around and hugged Dante, my unruly appearance and worry over not being able to transform forgotten.

"I just want to stand right here and hug you forever," I murmured, and leaned my head back to look him in the eye. "Promise you won't see me differently if this doesn't go well? I couldn't bear it if you thought less of me." I shuddered, hating the idea.

"You are my everything. How could I possibly think less of you? Now, we need to get a move on. It's nearly time." His phone rang and he left the bathroom to answer it.

My stomach churned, making me swallow hard. I straightened the front of my dress in the mirror and added another dozen bobby pins to my bun before I was satisfied it wouldn't fall down mid-way through the trial. *Trial.* That was exactly the way it felt to be hauled up in front of the tribunal, like I was going to be judged and sentenced.

"Ready to go?" Dante asked.

"You can do this," I said to my reflection, then went and joined him.

"The meeting is at the House of Anche, neutral territory for us."

I nodded, not trusting myself to speak. We exited the suite, followed by two burly bodyguards.

"It's not far," he said. We strode together down the long lushly carpeted corridors, taking an elevator that bore us down to the subterranean depths of Vegas.

Dante aggressively pushed open the glass doors to the Curia, a huge stone area that had obviously been made at great expense to duplicate the one from Ancient Rome and I strode in at his side. A large contingent of pack members were in attendance as well, seated on the sunken stone tiers, there to judge me, I imagined. Dante set his sights on the group of wolves gathered, addressing them.

"Welcome, my fellow Senators, and thank you for hearing our case today," he began. He had schooled me that they were all descended from ancient Roman royalty, three separate houses that sometimes warred, but that the Anche were known for neutrality and were often called upon to judge cases while the Ribelle were known troublemakers.

"It's come to our attention that a vampire is being chosen as a Forever Mate by Dante Luceres of the House of Luceres. Is this correct?" a tall, commanding man asked. Silver threaded his dark hair combed severely back from his face and his expression remained neutral, though I thought I could detect a note of scorn underlying his tone.

"No, that is not quite correct," Dante said, standing straight and true. "We don't choose our own Forever Mates, fate chooses. Amara St. Clair was brought to my attention the night she was attacked outside the Glitter Palace by an ancient foe, Pharoah Akar I, who had no regard for his actions."

"I have a document in front of me that says differently. It states he was given permission to find this human and make her a vampire."

"What? A human has no say in their own destiny?" I said, anger overcoming my better sense. "That's just wrong on every level. I love Dante. He rescued me, nursed me through a terrible illness that nearly took my life—that takes most human lives. Now I try to help him, volunteering to share my blood for his experiments to make shifters live longer."

"Is this true? Have you made a breakthrough?" The middle-aged man's eyes sharpened.

"I have." Dante nodded. "I intend to start trials very soon on a vaccine that can extend our lives, and it's all thanks to Amara, who so generously gave of herself even while she was recovering from a virus that left her terribly ill. It was touch and go for a number of days." He grabbed my hand and squeezed it, his expression telling of the worry and pain my being bitten had caused him.

"Do you have any other pertinent information for us to consider in our decision at this time? Before we invite Pharoah Akar to speak?" the judicator, Senatore Antonio asked, his expression not giving any clue to what he was thinking.

"As special compensation to Akar, I will offer the medicinal prescription that I designed to prevent the Bloodcall," Dante said. "I have proof that it works and will make it available to them at no expense."

A few positive nods came, but I had to persuade the jurors for certain. "Please, surely you understand about love? I love Dante Luceres more than life itself. I humbly prostrate myself before you, asking for what everyone else takes for granted. A life lived with someone I love deeply. Is that so much to ask?"

"I now call upon Pharoah Akar," Senatore Antonio said. "A warning—I have given my word that no one will attack him or his bodyguard while he attends this tribunal. Is that clear?"

No one said anything, but every eye turned and watched the group of vampires all dressed in black come into the ring from another door. They fanned out, adding a dark menacing presence to the event.

Cold chills crept down my spine. *Love is all*, I reminded myself. Surely love can fix this?

"I, Akar the first, demand my bride be returned to me," he said, his cruel mouth downturned with disgust while his nostrils flared. "I am unwilling to accept any kind of payment in lieu of what I am owed. Amara St. Claire was promised to me, a reincarnation of my lost love."

"I will never turn Amara over to you. I will see you burn in hellfire first!" Dante said, his powerful voice ringing out in the tight quarters.

"Wait! It is too late for this. I am already claimed by Dante. I let him bite me recently," I said.

"Is this true?" the senator asked.

"Yes," Dante said.

"I don't believe it! Make her change to a wolf, prove it!" Akar demanded. "Otherwise, I am taking her with me. Now!"

"Never! You lay one finger on her and so help me God I will not be accountable for what I do," Dante promised.

"I will allow Amara to prove her ability for the court. If she can become one of us this day, become a wolf, then she stays with Dante," Senatore Antonia announced.

My heart sank. Change to wolf? All was lost if I could not do this thing. I couldn't bear the thought of a minute away from Dante, let alone a lifetime that never ended. That would be the worst of punishments. A torture beyond the keen.

"I will do it," I said though my mind screamed *how?* Dante gave me a strained look, knowing my failure to date. "But does Akar promise to let me go and to leave us in peace when I do?" *Please let me be able to do this*, I begged the goddess.

"I will accept other payment. The formula to ease the Bloodcall."

"So be it," Senatore Antonio said, bringing down his gavel.

"Quick. Give me your blood," I whispered in Dante's ear. "That's our only hope. I am prepared to die if I can't change. I beg you, do this thing. I just need the real thing, not that sterilized substitute you make in the lab."

He did as I bid then, tearing his wrist open and applying it to my lips, sending a few drops of rich blood onto my tongue, so fast that I was feeling the charge to my system before anyone was the wiser. But then why should they care? Blood shared was common, between consenting adults.

"Envision yourself a wolf. See the world as a wolf would. Feel the wolf within," Dante counseled.

I listened to him with all my being, trying to see myself as wolf.

"Watch me." Dante waited for the shimmer to occur the nanosecond before the portal to next door opened in a blaze of light and I watched him step through it. He came back as wolf, his 'shift' instant.

He pushed his nose into my hand, asking in the most ancient way, "*Join me.*"

"Believe me, I want to," I answered.

An implosion of air knocked us against each other. Dante growled, alert.

"What's happening?"

"*Stay behind me,*" Dante urged.

"Isn't this a pretty picture?" Akar sneered, stepping in front of us, his bodyguards gone.

Then I realized the entire world had changed all around us. No longer were the tribunal members present, but just the three of us. What magic had created this? Were we on a different plane and not on earth? Another dimension? Did that make any sense? Yeah, about as much sense of being turned into a vampire. *No fighting this new reality.*

"I thought it best we settle this alone without all those dogs present. So, you betrayed my kindness," Akar said, staring at me. "Poor choice you made, the cur over a pharaoh who would have given you the world."

"He's not a cur and you're not a pharaoh anymore — this isn't ancient Egypt — but a fucking cold psychopath who gets his kicks out of torturing innocent women."

"Why don't you say what you really think," Akar said with a curl of his lip, a malicious glint in his obsidian eyes.

"Leave us alone. You've done enough harm for one lifetime," I said.

"No, not nearly enough. I want to see both of you pay for this disrespect. I thought the tribunal would have more teeth, send you both packing. But now I see I'm the one who will have to dispense real justice."

"Justice? You freak! If there was any justice you'd be tossed into a silver-lined box and hidden deep in the bowels of the earth."

"*Shift. Now.*" Dante's voice filled my head.

"No luck as a wolf?" Akar said with a sneer, coming closer. "Leaves you rather vulnerable. My blood is obviously stronger than the dog's."

"*See your wolf. Fight for what is yours. There's no more time, Amara.*"

I felt ill. My body trembled. I grabbed handfuls of his fur.

"*Breathe. Don't see him. See us, together. Running side-by-side, free.*"

There was a slight shimmering, a stirring of the air.

"*Yes, keep at it. You're almost there.*"

A brighter shimmering and I vanished into the abyss.

"Where did she go?" Akar asked me, his expression stunned as his eyes darted back and forth looking for Amara.

I kept a close watch on Akar, waiting for him to attack.

"*Where are you?*" I asked, concerned when Amara didn't reappear immediately. Never before had this happened. My species came back as a wolf right away, no lingering on the other side.

"I don't know. It's beautiful though. All wildflowers and colorful butterflies and a waterfall beside a fragrant meadow. Is this heaven?"

"No, Summerland. Come back to me."

"I'm trying!"

"Where the fuck is Amara?" Akar demanded, frowning.

As a wolf, I could not answer him. Instead, I growled in warning.

For the first time the vampire looked uncertain, obviously unsure of what to do. I had to finish this. I moved forward, ready to fight the cold one, my fur on end, growling louder to voice my intent.

"Fuck this!" Akar flew at me, his body airborne before landing behind me and spinning around to kick out with his feet, landing a solid blow to my ribs.

I ignored the instant pain and went for the most vulnerable part of any creature, their neck. I grasped the foul one between my powerful jaws, holding on tight, ready to suffocate the life right out of Akar. Akar wasn't done yet. He shoved a fist into my chest, sending a rush of air to escape, then spun away when my hold lessened.

"Try that again, dog," Akar boasted, his expression maniacal.

Before Akar could react, I was on him. This time my bite was true, right down to the backbones on the creature's neck. The sound of bones snapping, then the monster lay still, his black blood dripping onto the ground. But it wasn't over yet.

Never turn your back on a vampire.

I held on, waiting until the last drop of blood quit flowing, then I shook the body until the head snapped free.

Chapter Twenty-Eight

Amara

I stopped trying to leave and sat by the waterfall, mesmerized by the silvery white water. I cupped my hands together under the flow and brought some of the sweet nectar to my mouth. It was refreshing and tasty, like the best vitamin additive ever.

Summerland was so beautiful. I couldn't imagine why I would ever want to leave. Oh, right, someone waited for me on the other side. Who was that?

How long had I been here? The birdsong remained the same, the temperature perfect. I drifted in my mind, slowly pulled along by a current that sucked me inward to where there was no need to worry, no need to fight for anything.

"Amara, come back to me!"

Who was talking to me? My eyes were so heavy, I didn't want to disturb them.

"Isn't this the most beautiful place on earth?"

"*Yes, but you have to leave, my love. You're in mortal danger.*"

"Danger? No, there's no danger here. All that is back on earth. That's where the danger lies."

"*If you don't leave right now, you'll be forced to stay there for all eternity. Without me, Dante, your Forever Mate.*"

"Dante?" I tried very hard to focus on his words.

"Yes, the man who loves science."

"*The man who loves you very deeply and is worried to death about you. You need to come to me. Now. I would die without you, Amara, but I can't stay in Summerland. No pure wolf can.*"

"Okay, if it's so important to you, I'll try."

I got up reluctantly, uncertain it couldn't be so vital that one would need to leave such a wondrous place. But the man loved me, wanted to be with me, and something deep inside said I must go to him, I must break free. I tried focusing hard on going back. My mind hurt when I tried, but something made me try harder.

His image came to me then, a bright aura around him, a shininess that spoke of his essence. Yes, I felt the love. What was I doing in this place? I wanted to go home.

"*Amara, come to me. Feel my love.*"

I tried again, seeing myself with my love. I shook my head, a sudden implosion of images burning its way through my brain. I screamed in pain. "What's happening to me? Make it stop!" I needed to break free of this. I pushed so hard, I felt something snap deep inside me. All my bones seemed to fly apart, rearrange themselves. Then I was free!

I slumped onto the ground, confused. Then the fog lifted…and I realized I was a wolf too! Not only that, but we were back at the tribunal, surrounded by Luceres and Anche wolves.

"*Oh my God. Am I really here? I was so far away, but everything's come back to me. Oh Dante, I love you so much. Aww, but you've been hurt.*" Blood on his fur upset me. I looked at my coat and saw it was golden, such a pretty color.

"*I'm fine. I took care of Akar. There was a battle. He's gone forever.*"

"*Oh, thank you. Those are wonderful words to hear.*"

"*We're free now, sweetheart. Free to live our lives without regret or looking over our shoulders.*"

"*I did it. I'm a wolf.*"

"*Yes, you are. A beautiful wolf. Thank you for loving me,*" Dante said simply, bringing tears to my eyes.

"*Believe me, the pleasure's all mine,*" I said, stroking his face with my tongue. "*Or it will be later,*" I teased, wanting to see the rise I would get and not being at all disappointed at his instant attention.

"*We'll see what we can do.*"

The loud sound of a gavel hitting a wooden surface three times drew both our attention. "It is the decision of this court that Dante of the House of Luceres and Amara St. Clair can be united in a Forever Mate union. May no wolf tear it asunder. Now, shall we adjourn for the celebration?"

A loud cheer rose at the welcome words.

"*No worries. I can wait a bit longer. After all, we've got a lifetime, plus who knows how long ahead of us? And I could really use a party about now…that's if I can shift back to human,*" I said, thinking of our formula now completed and proven to work without any adverse side effects to the test subjects so far. A half-dozen shifters plus ourselves were now blessed with all of eternity. Sure, challenges lay ahead, but with endless time to correct things, I could only imagine the good works we could accomplish for humanity and supernaturals alike.

"I'll help you with that. You'll be a pro before you know it. By the way, the Amara-Eternity drug works perfectly, meaning endless good times to come, that I can promise."

"You've named it! Amara-Eternity, huh. I like the sound of that. Say, do you think the drug might work on Rainbow and Shay?"

"Maybe. That remains to be seen. But we'll give it our best shot."

I looked up into his beautiful eyes, dreaming of the future. The best was yet to be. I had a sudden inspiration. Something I wanted to do more than anything.

"Let's run together."

"You're on. But first you must change back so that we can head into the desert by helicopter. I know all the best spots."

My throat tightened. Could I do it?

Yes. A couple of seconds later, I was in human form again and quickly re-dressed with Dante shielding my body from view. In reality, the shift to wolf or human was easy to explain. Unique DNA had been turned on in some bloodlines and allowed them to become altered at the quantum, or sub-atomic, level into pure energy. As energy cannot be destroyed, only altered, they could shift from pure energy into a new form at the quantum level.

But who really cared about all that mumbo jumbo when it meant I could be with Dante, as wolf or human?

We raced out of the Curia, hand in hand, headed for the roof of the Glitter Palace. Then a short copter ride later, we were in the desert, surrounded by Joshua trees, thick tumbleweeds and tons of sand.

We jumped out of the helicopter and lay our clothes aside. Naked, we made the switch to wolf. Now for some fun!

I nipped at Dante's muzzle, then took off at great speed, enticing him to follow me. The air rushed by me as the summer wind ruffled my thick fur and gave life to all my senses. We ran for miles, our powerful bodies, so long and lean, capable of great feats as we danced among the dunes of sand. I could see for miles, detect the odor of every creature on the breeze, feel the heartbeat of the earth beneath my paws.

Dante shimmered back to human form. I did as well. We lay together by a stream of artisan water that formed a small bubbling pool, the babbling sound sweet music. We mated, our bodies sliding easily into each other, as natural as breathing. When we finished, we lay and watched the California stars that glowed down, anointing us with their light.

"Ready for that family celebration now, sweetheart? The pack is looking forward to welcoming you into the fold." Dante pushed a lock of hair back from my face, trapping it behind my ear. "Every moment with you is a celebration," he said. "Thank you for choosing me. You've made me the happiest man on earth."

"No person could be happier at this moment than me. I love you, Dante Luceres, with all my heart and soul," I swore.

"I love you, sweetheart, with all that I am, and all that I will be, for all eternity."

Oh, it didn't get any finer than that. A lifetime without restrictions, with a man I loved more than anything and who I would love for all eternity.

I smiled, and Dante smiled back.

Want to see more from this author?
Here's a taster for you to enjoy!

Sin City Kilts: Heart of Stone
January Bain

Coming Spring 2023

Excerpt

Lachlan

I jumped naked from my bed, the stone floor bracing against my bare feet and the early morning chill raising quick goosebumps on my flesh. The clash of sword and shouts of men I led into battle nightly in my dreams still rang in my ears before I stretched and let the images fade away.

Last night's full moon still lingered and false dawn approached, that luminal moment when the sun has yet to appear. My ancestors believed it heralded glimpses of the future and great secrets to be shared. Me? I thought it time to be up and about.

Throwing on my shirt, kilt and boots then strapping my claymore to my back, I descended the steep steps from the north tower. Despite myself, I sensed something of import with the night's Hawthorn moon—a time of masculine power, potency and fertility, even more so than the other eleven months of the year.

Fingers of heavy mist crept across the vast estate toward me, intensifying the fresh woodsy scents of heather and moss. The low-lying fog obscured my long view of forest and hedgerows, but I knew they were there.

Untold numbers of Creigs had carved this land and battlements out of solid rock eons ago on *Eilean maddah-allaidh* or Wolf Island as it was known to those from away, creating a legacy that would stand for generations to come. A sanctuary that was mine to oversee and care for…which included being alive to any messages sent my way.

"Okay, fine," I sighed to whoever or whatever might be listening, and, giving in, stood outside in the shadow of Castle Creigbourne, awaiting a glimpse of what lay beyond the ken.

An intense flickering in my peripheral vision hit my senses hard before the world disappeared entirely, sending me back to that timeless realm with no name and no season. Then a glimmering of light appeared as my third eye opened, sending flashes of blue and gold to strike my retinas. The blue of eyes and the gold of hair?

I grasped for more but the partial image vanished in an instant. "That all?" I snarked, shaking off the disquiet that the vision left in its wake. No answer came. Shrugging, I strode across the ground toward the stables. The first rays of light glinted on the dewy grass now as the sun returned, creating a field of ephemeral sparkling diamonds that never failed to put all human efforts to shame.

A series of soft chuffs broke the quiet stillness as Loki came trotting over to greet me. The legendary deerhound voted most likely to be mistaken for a large pony swiped his tail to a steady beat.

"Ah, this is the time we like best, isn't it, my Loki boy?" I asked, bending to give his thick, wiry fur a quick rub.

He followed me into the stable, sneezing as the sharp scent of manure tickled his nose. I opened the door to Roam's stall, then led the magnificent stallion out into the alleyway and swiftly saddled him. The scent of oiled leather and clean horse flesh permeated the air, grounding me.

I swung a leg up and over the coal black beast, both of us impatient to be off. Roam stomped the hard ground with loud thumps of his massive hoofs. A thoroughbred, he was of sturdy stock with bloodlines that harked back to tournament fields and knights in amour. He needed to be to carry the likes of this Highlander — six-foot-three of solid muscle, thanks to the daily regime of the claymore.

"Let's go."

A loud whinny of agreement followed, the stallion's breath whitening the brisk air in pillowy clouds as we surged away from Castle Creigbourne. I gave Roam his head and we raced across the glen, Loki running along by our side, the three of us as ancient as any legend.

"Creigbourne Loch?" I suggested.

Roam knew the way and barely needed my touch on the reins before his strong haunches were chewing up the miles across a greenscape as brilliant as existed on planet Earth.

The clean air and the colors of nature worked their usual wonder on me and helped to place the morning's vision in perspective. "Second sight is sometimes a gift, sometimes a curse," I told my animals. Which was the hazy impression sent to me this morning? The blue and gold could be either, depending on opinion.

Blue eyes, gold hair... Personally, I was not looking for the female prophesized by the elderly woman at last year's Spirit of Creigbourne festival. I had no need of distraction. My life in the Highlands of Scotland was filled with dealing with the needs of my clan, and I'd have it no other way. Family honor and loyalty was everything.

The edge of the loch loomed and I dismounted. Tugging my shirt over my head, I threw it on the ground and took up my broadsword.

Swiping and lunging at demons and enemies, I cut a swathe across the clearing. Under the canopy of forest, I swung the claymore with precision and speed, savoring the perfectly balanced weapon in my hand. It was born of the finest steel and crafted with such remarkable precision that I'd been offered a king's ransom for its possession. *Never.* Not enough money on this earth to entice me to part with the pride of the Creig clan.

An hour later, my bare chest dripping with perspiration that pooled in the ridges and valleys of my fairly earned six-pack, I removed my sturdy boots and kilt and dived into the frigid waters of Creigbourne Loch.

Sluicing back my long hair from my face, I swam out a fair distance from the rocky shore, enjoying the pull on muscles that were well-used from my workout. A bark from Loki and a whinny from Roam alerted me a second before a long-winged shadow skimmed across the water. I stilled, treading in place for a moment to observe the interloper. *Tyr.* Damn, the falcon was even now about to disturb my peace.

The fierce falcon, named Tyr after a special god of bravery—a nod to my ancient Norse ancestors and to The Creig—settled on a rock nearby, his golden eyes beady and ever watchful. Then with a series of proud screeches to announce his presence and departure, the giant bird of prey flapped his shoulders, rising into the air on powerful wings meant to catch the wind current home or to hunt.

I swam swiftly to shore and pulled on my boots. Wrapping my kilt around my waist, uncaring of my wet skin, I whistled for Roam and Loki. "Time to head in. We have a visitor," I told them.

The ride back to the castle was all too short. I curried Roam and fed him fresh carrots on top of his full share of oats and nutrients, making sure the stallion had all his needs met before heading into the conservatory where the visitor whose herald had summoned me held court.

I rolled my shoulders, the unease of dealing with whatever had prompted the visit bringing back the tension that my early morning exercise had almost eliminated. I had no choice on the matter though — when *this* visitor called, any Creig with a whit of sense answered.

I girded my loins and strode in the doorway. "Morning, Grandmother."

"Morning, Grandson," The Creig, the elder of the clan, said, turning her stately head with its elegant upswept hairdo to present her cheek for my buss. Dressed in the customary Creigbourne tartan of black and green plaid with gold threads running through it, she perched on her throne, slight enough to be blown away in a stiff breeze. However, no one in their right mind would dare even *think* that.

"Ye're soaking wet, Lachlan. Dinna ye think to bring a towel?"

I laughed. "No need. I have the constitution of an ox, the strength of a bull and the fortitude of a conqueror. Why waste time?"

"And the lasses in these parts would add...and a heart of stone," she said, then added, "Aye, but yer right, it's precious it is. Time. Never enough of it."

She nodded sagely, her piercing green eyes still not requiring correction though she was ninety if she were a day. No woman admits her age, according to The Creig. She'd been thirty-nine forever before she finally quit discussing the matter entirely. Her birthday cake was only allowed one candle to this day.

"What brings you here on this fine morning?" I asked though a pall had been laid over the day. I sat down across from her. *Might as well get it over with.* The Creig never showed up unless something difficult was afoot. Unease reared itself in my mind, making my nerves rankle. I damn well knew the next words out of her mouth would annoy me, would have a cost.

"Ye are needed in America, Grandson. Cristaldo of the House of Luceres has asked for our help in a personal matter and has a business opportunity he wishes to discuss. It is time to pay our debt."

She looked at me more keenly when I remained stubbornly silent. I detested owing a duty. So often the wishes of another burdened beyond compare.

"But I see ye already knew something of this." She pursed her lips. "If ye second sight is talking to ye, then it's settled."

I ignored her last words, pushed myself out of the chair and began to pace. I preferred to think on my feet. "I have a great deal on my plate at the moment, taking care of our vast holdings. I can't just rush off to America at the whim of another."

I was venting, knowing I would have to answer the call. As head of the clan, paying the ancient debt the Greigs owed to the house of Luceres fell to me, and I would honor that, not even think about sending my younger brothers Calan or Logan, or even one of our cousins.

"I knew it would come to this one day, but not now," I muttered. A warrior chooses his own path, his own battles. Of course, once I wanted something, I would not be deterred from obtaining it by any means necessary. How else could I have doubled our billions in the past decade alone? "But, of course, honor above all."

"Aye." The Creig picked up her dram of spirits she'd poured earlier. She swallowed it a single gulp. "Spectacular year."

"It is." I waited for her to come to the point.

"Was your vision any clearer this morn?" Her question hung in the air between us, those few words filled with more portent than the most dramatic soliloquy and, knowing what she was asking, I shook my head, a bit more riled than I let on.

She leaned forward to add weight to her words. "Well, ye must think of the future, grandson. Ye are heir to all we possess, as is the right of the first born. And ye are not getting any younger." She pointed her glass at me. "And neither am I. Would you deny me grandchildren?"

I snorted. "You're going to live forever. And it's blatantly unfair, the structure of inheritance. Archaic laws that need changing."

"Be that as it may, if ye canna find your mate on this side of the water, she may exist in the new world."

Her words clanged like warning bells, especially when allied to the reason for her visit. "Grandmother,

I'm not looking to upend my life. A lass from another country with a different culture causes too many complications. I have too many responsibilities right here. Obligations that cannot be set aside on the whim of another."

"We must learn from the past, but embrace the present, Grandson. You won't be the first to cross the water for your mate, your one. Besides, it might lighten ye up!"

I grimaced and let The Creig's words sink in as she poured us both a drink of Scotland's finest. My life was so regimented, the needs of others firmly set before my own, as it should be for the alpha of a clan, one who needed to lighten Grandmother's load as she aged.

And yes, over the quickly passing years, I had become less light-hearted and more solemn, though the love of wit and laughter called strongly at times. Things an adult must set aside. *Isn't that the proper way of it? Not kicking over the traces?*

I glanced at my favorite painting of all time that hung on the conservatory's wall. Backlit spectacularly by the artist, it depicted my great-grandfather doing a sleight-of-hand magic trick, a gaggle of his grandchildren huddled by his feet, their tiny faces alight with amazement. I'd always been fascinated by stories of him, and his personality.

Then, as if he were calling to me, a thought struck me. If I had to visit Las Vegas, or Sin City as it was more rightly called, maybe I could recapture something of my lighter side, and do something I'd always wanted to do? Take, some recompense for the interruption to my life? Could I? *Yes.*

"Fine. But I get to do it my way." I said, crossing my arms over my chest.

The Greig's eyes gleamed with interest and she stared at me, but I remained stubbornly silent. *Where do you think I got my need to turn the world my way?* She tilted her head, as if listening to something I couldn't hear, then nodded. "Good. It's settled then. Now, how about some breakfast?"

Taken aback, I muttered, "Of course," and mulled over the situation while we ate the tempting dishes the servants brought at her request. I quickly consumed vast quantities of steak and bacon, sausage and eggs with sides of toast and oatcakes in short order. I had a great deal of preparing to do and little time to accomplish it.

"If you'll excuse me, I have somewhere I need to be."

The Greig nodded as I took my leave, her expression expressing pleasure at the outcome of our meeting. As if it were ever in doubt. I always uphold the honor of our family.

"Off with ye, grandson. I look forward to my invite."

The Greig had passed the second sight on to me, the first born, though her advancing years had added immeasurably to her ability. She knew far more than she would ever admit about what awaited me in Vegas, but it would be no use asking her to divulge it, and I was too proud to beg.

Exiting the castle, I tore off my kilt and boots, ready for my real exercise — my wolf run. Creigs were weres, our secret ancestral heritage, and this would be my last chance before heading off to Sin City. I wanted it to count. I wanted to feel the wind in my fur, the scent of life in my lungs and the world dropping away as I raced across the moors.

I pushed my way from our realm through the glimmering portal into the next dimension so tantalisingly close to ours, the process necessary to shift my energy from man to wolf, the actual transformation occurring in an instant. All those painful experiences expressed in novels? Patently untrue for any werewolf I knew, which was a small mercy.

The world had now mutated to an array of colors unknown to the human eye, blacks and browns and grays with subtle shadings that my brain converted to what my human side saw—blues and greens, yellow and reds. I breathed in deeply, my olfactory nerves sharpened by the cool, moist morning Highland air, each scent more rousing than the last.

A chorus of howls erupted in the distance, begging me to join them. I took off at a quick lope, overcome with a sense of urgency. This might be my last chance for a while.

I slipped off the bonds of duty, my worries over the Creig estate and concerns about the journey to America. Instead, I embraced my animal nature, letting it take over. The grasses compressed beneath my massive paws, acting like a springboard to my prowling.

I stood taller and larger than the thought-to-be-extinct dire wolf and, blessed with sharper tracking ability, soon picked up the scent trail of Calan and Logan.

Around a thick stand of birch and oak trees, I caught sight of them with my superior vision, my younger brothers lying in ambush, hoping to catch me unaware. My wolf mouth stretched in a grin.

I'd teach them a thing or two.

About the Author

January Bain has wished on every falling star, every blown-out birthday candle and every coin thrown in a fountain to be a storyteller. To share the tales of high adventure, mysteries, and full-blown thrillers she has dreamed of all her life. The story you now have in your hands is the compilation of a lot of things manifesting itself for this special series. Hundreds of hours spent researching the unusual and the mundane have come together to create a series that features strong women who don't take life too seriously, wild adventures full of twists and unforeseen turns, and hot complicated men who aren't afraid to take risks. She can only hope the stories of her beloved Brass Ringers will capture your imagination as much as they did hers when she wrote them.

If you are looking for January Bain, you can find her hard at work every morning without fail in her office with two furry babies trying to prove who does a better job of guarding the doorway. And, of course, she's married to the most romantic man! Who once famously replied to her inquiry about buying fresh flowers for their home every week, "Give me one good reason why not?" Leaving her speechless and knocking her head against the proverbial wall for being so darn foolish. She loves flowers.

January loves to hear from readers. You can find her contact information, website details and author profile page at https://www.totallybound.com

Home of Erotic Romance

Sign up for our newsletter and find out about all our romance book releases, eBook sales and promotions, sneak peeks and FREE romance books!

www.ingramcontent.com/pod-product-compliance
Lightning Source LLC
Chambersburg PA
CBHW050734180626
46814CB00002B/742